THE MAP MAKER'S SISTER

THE
MAP MAKER'S
SISTER

Matthew J. Krengel

NORTH STAR PRESS OF ST. CLOUD, INC.
Saint Cloud, Minnesota

First Edition: September 2013

Printed in the United States of America

Published by
North Star Press of St. Cloud, Inc.
P.O. Box 451
St. Cloud, Minnesota 56302

THE MAP MAKER'S SISTER

PROLOGUE

"MASTER CAIN?"

The thin dwarf turned and looked to where the much taller human was running down the hallway towards where he was standing. He waited until the man stumbled to a halt and bowed before motioning him to continue with whatever was troubling him. These humans sometimes needed reminding of the power structure inside the Temple of Adherency.

"What is it?" Cain asked calmly, anxious to continue but knowing minor delays were expected as his influence expanded across the new world.

"We lost contact with two of our runners over the last day."

"You interrupted me for that?" Cain asked with a raised eyebrow. "How many times do I need to tell you it matters little how many we send. As long as the flow of materials and information keeps moving I don't care how many we train and send."

"But sire," the man continued. "One of them reported seeing your old mentor before he disappeared. He is on the other side of the Divide."

Cain's eyes lit up briefly, "So that's where he's been hiding. I had wondered, but I doubted he had the courage to try to hide on the other side. Perfect then. He's out of our way for now and most likely searching for his next Map Maker and Runner to send against me." Cain smiled wickedly as he thought about the last two his mentor had sent to their demise. One was still locked in the deepest dungeon, lined with cold iron walls, and unconnected to any map anywhere. The other had been lost to the Divide. Oh, he knew another Map Maker and Runner moved about in the human world, but he had his leverage if they became an issue. Even if they came against him, he held the trump cards against them.

"Yes, sire. I'll send out two more the moment ' medallions are done."

"What of the girl we took last year," Cain asked suddenly. "Where is she being held? We know that Tasker was interested in her. I wonder if he knows that we took her?"

1

"She resisted all our attempts to recruit to our side," the man replied. "We sent her to the Isle of Lakes to be held there in case we needed her. Viscount Lerod is still hoping you'll forget about her so he can take her for himself."

"Perfect," Cain muttered. "She'll be well protected there. Tell the viscount to keep his distance from her though." He waved his hand to the human still standing with his head bowed before him. He knew the man was watching despite doing his best to look as though he wasn't. "You may go." Cain continued down the corridor until he reached the furthest end of the passage and stopped before an ornately carved door made of solid mahogany. The handles were bronze and inlaid with a type of gold that glowed with a coppery hue. He slipped inside the room and took a deep breath. The area was filled with book shelves weighted down with volumes. Slowly he walked around the outside of the shelves and let his eyes travel across the bound leather spines. All this knowledge and still he was missing the very item he craved.

In the center of the room a wide circle of stones marked off a charred area. It suddenly blazed to life, flames of every color of the rainbow leaping and crackling with magical power. The fire required no fuel—the blaze was drawn from the interplay of the magnetic fields surrounding the world and other mysterious sources.

"Right on time," Cain muttered. He had spent the last five weeks laying the ground work in the mountain city of Denver and now it was coming to fruition. What a delightfully perfect plan for removing items of knowledge from those who didn't need them and still preserving the knowledge for himself. He could see it in his mind, the fires leaping high as his Adherents tossed arm loads of parchment- and leather-bound volumes into the blaze. He could hear the cheers of the onlookers, goaded by his men walking the perimeter of the throng, their fingers dangerously near their weapons' triggers. His hands twitched as the first of the books materialized inside the magical flames and slowly floated over to where he stood. Carefully, he set it off to the side and waited as more continued to come through the magical flames.

* * * * *

Two months earlier

JACKIE STUMBLED INTO THE CELL and glared back at the guard who had shoved her. He smirked back at her and then slammed the door shut and she heard the lock turn. Almost a year since she had gone running down by the Mississippi River back in St Paul. Four men in black robes grabbed her as she entered a small stand of trees that shaded the running trail on each side. She fought for she was worth but they bound her hands and pinned a strange amulet to her chest. Moments later the world vanished and suddenly she was here in this strange world. At first they had treated her well and some short guy had tried to be her friend, when she had refused to help him the guy turned nasty. So here she sat, locked in a small room wondering if anyone even remembered her any more. She sat down on the edge of her wooden bunk and slumped down into the filthy mattress. A few tears slipped down her cheek but she pushed them away and finally lay down on her bed. No one was coming for her. Sometime later there was a tap at the door and a young man slipped inside the door holding a tray of food.

"What do you want?" Jackie asked wearily.

"Just dropping off some food for you."

Jackie glared at him but did not sit up, "I am not helping you."

"I didn't ask you to."

Jackie sat up slowly and took a better look at him. He looked like he was the same age as she was and he had an unruly shock of black hair that perched atop his head. His clothes were finely made and cleaner than other soldiers she had seen. She thought his face was nice and he had a natural smile that made her feel good.

"Do you want to eat?"

Jackie swung her legs over the edge of the bunk and shrugged, "It doesn't make a difference. You will never let me go back to my family."

"I really am sorry about that," he paused as he leaned against the wall next to the door. "My name is Carvin, I wish I could change what happened."

"Just go away," Jackie muttered.

* * * * *

Present day

TASKER SAT INSIDE the smallest of the structures, the buildings surrounded by the rough timber walls that protected the fort on Stockton Island. Outside he could hear shouts and sound of hammers as the damaged sections of the palisade were repaired and the remaining sections re-enforced to withstand whatever would be thrown at them. He shuddered as he thought about the things he had seen humans do on the other side of the Divide. Were that technology to come here and be made to operate, all of his hard work would be lost in a few nights.

"Are you going to tell her when she comes back?" Eriunia asked from where she sat across the table. The tall elf was clothed in a sturdy wool tunic and soft leather pants, her feet protected by doeskin boots and her black hair tied back in a tight ponytail. Large green eyes turned and examined Bella where the fairy fluttered back and forth in a nervous fashion across the table from Puck. *What an odd grouping they made*, the elf thought. The fairy who just wants to gain her family back, the hobgoblin who would do anything to be king of his own land, myself who just wants to go home, and the enigmatic dwarf who'd had it all, lost it, and now seemed bent on repaying his debt. However, in Tasker's case, the dwarf was acting completely different from what he had been. *How does one go from a founding member of the Seely Court and meddling in the affairs of people everywhere to leading a rebellion against a religious order he helped found?* The affairs of men and dwarf were hard to comprehend.

"What? I should tell her I made a mistake?" Tasker muttered. "No, the history is behind us, leave it there." He looked down at the table and closed his eyes for a moment as if in deep thought. "We can take Madeline Island and our position here will be more secure than before. If we are careful and use the element of surprise, we can also have possession of the Ironships currently stationed there."

"You know that once we take those ships, it's only a matter of time before Cain knows something's wrong and sends out either the fleet at Isle of Lakes, or, in a worst-case scenario, he'll send the Lake Huron fleet north through the straights," Puck stated. He sat back in his chair and wrapped his hands behind his head. He leaned back further in his chair using his furry goat legs to support the front of the chair as he leaned his weight on the back legs.

"I have some ideas, but it requires that we move quickly and with as much stealth as possible," Tasker replied. He was the second shortest of the beings present but had, at one time, wielded considerable power.

"Are you going to tell us?" Bella asked. She fluttered down to the table top and sat down with her tiny legs crossed. The bow and quiver that Yerdarva the Red had given her lay carefully across her legs. The tiny fairy was extremely proud of the weapon and had put it to good use in the last series of skirmishes that cleared many of the Prison Islands and added almost two thousand rebels to Tasker's forces. She wondered how many they'd free as the larger islands to the south were taken.

"Keep in mind that my people will not become involved unless my three sisters are found and released from their captivity." Eriunia reminded Tasker. "I wish it were not so, but my father will not risk any of their lives for what he certainly views as a problem for the Seely Court and the committees to deal with."

"And what of you, Eriunia?" Tasker asked. "Is this a problem that you will ignore given the chance?"

Her eyes flashed as they narrowed, and her jaw was set in a firm line, "I am still here, am I not?"

"Good," Tasker said. "I need those who are dedicated to this cause."

"How like the message you started with a few hundred years ago," Puck said slyly as he looked at Tasker out of the corner of his eyes, but the dwarf ignored him and continued planning.

"When Jane and Jacob return, I want our people in place. I believe it's possible to take Madeline Island without a battle, but I must work out certain things with those two alone in order for the plan to work."

"And what shall we do while we wait?" Bella piped out in her high-pitched voice.

"Make sure we've checked every corner of the islands we've freed," Tasker ordered as he stood, bringing his head and shoulders just above the table. "I don't want any to be left behind if they wish to escape. Offer a place to anyone who wants to get on the ships."

Puck nodded, "I'll send messengers to every island."

"Ferry them all here. When the time comes, we'll leave from here," Tasker said and the hobgoblin nodded again. Tasker left the table and walked down the short hall to where two of the Adherents were still locked in the holding cell. Both of them looked up at him as he opened the door. They glared at him angrily. He motioned the two rebels standing guard to leave, and then stepped into the cell and looked down at the chained men.

"Has he found what he seeks?" Tasker asked quietly. He alone believed he knew what Cain truly sought—something that in his younger days he had sought as well. The obsession with certain ancient artifacts of great evil had led Tasker to banish Cain from his presence and then had led to the current strife. Some things in this world should never again be found.

"What are you talking about, little dwarf," the bigger of the two men spat back. "Free us, and I will show you how Adherents treats traitors to the cause." He struggled against the chains, then sank back to the floor.

Tasker took a step closer and narrowed his eyes. A glint of steel crossed his face as he leaned close and smiled at the man, "I can send you into the Divide forever if you want."

"Go ahead and try," the prisoner blustered. "You wouldn't dare."

The man gasped as Tasker's hand flashed out and grabbed the man's wrist. Tasker reached into his belt and pulled an old worn anchor from his pocket. He poked the prisoner's hand with the pin and smiled at him.

"Last chance to answer me," he said with dark warning.

"Never," the man spat back angrily.

"So be it," Tasker muttered. "I hope someday when I am called to Task for my life and choices I can find a suitable reason for this.

A flash of darkness surrounded the man, and Tasker pulled the anchor back at the last moment. A look of surprise filled the man's face as the darkness closed in around him. Then he was gone. All that remained were the chains, which, now empty, fell to the floor with a clunk.

Tasker turned to the to the smaller of the Adnerents. "Now, what about you . . . will you answer my questions?"

"I . . . I don't think he's found it yet," the Adherent said slowly as he stared at the floor where his fellow soldier had sat only moments before.

"If he had, something would have been said, but the orders are always the same. For the missionaries, find him new places to visit and bring back word of any collections of books for him to burn."

Tasker turned and left the room only slighty happier than when he entered. What he had done to the first adherent prisoner was akin to murder, and it made him feel dirty inside. Still, he thought he alone knew what Cain's true purpose was. Knowledge of that made him ready to do almost anything to stop his former pupil.

"Does that make me any better than he is?" Tasker asked himself quietly. To that question he had no answers.

CHAPTER ONE

Rude Awakenings

DULUTH, MINNESOTA, WAS QUIET for the first time in days. On-going rescue efforts continued, but nothing out of place had happened for almost a full day, and many residents breathed a sigh of relief. It had been the strangest beginning to a summer most would ever remember, starting with a number of rogue waves rising out of Lake Superior and rumors of local citizens being attacked and suspects disappearing from police custody.

Grandpa Able looked up from the paper and frowned, when some-one knocked on the front door with an insistent rap. He stood and shuf-fled to the door. At eight in the evening, he couldn't think of anyone who should be visiting. The front door, a grand wood and glass affair, allowed him at least a glance of who was standing on the porch. His heart beat a little faster when he saw the emblem of the Duluth police department through the smudged glass. Slowly he pulled the door open and looked out at the grim-faced officer. He immediately took a dislike to the man who wore a uniform two sizes too big for him and a face that looked like it hadn't been shaved in weeks. Coffee and food stains on the white cot-ton neckline of his under shirt bothered him, and the officer's hat was tilted downward to shadow his eyes.

"What can I do for you, sir?" Grandpa Able asked quietly, putting his feelings aside and framing his words in the most polite voice possible.

"Is this the residence of Jane Timbrill?" the officer asked in a dead voice. He glanced up and narrowed his eyes at Grandpa Able.

"Yes, it is," Grandpa Able replied. His heart began to beat even faster as he wondered what had happened. If anything happened to the girl while she was here, he would never forgive himself, not after what the family had been through when her older sister had disappeared. That whole affair had ended with the divorce of Jane's parents and her father leaving the state to return to his family's home in Colorado. Jane didn't like to talk about it, but he knew it hurt her horribly.

"Is she here?" the officer casually set his hand on his utility belt as he asked the question. His fingers tapped slowly on the leather as he waited for the answer.

"No, she went hiking up the North Shore with a friend," Grandpa Able replied. He disliked the officer even more as the man tried to inch his way forward and look into the house. "Is there something wrong?"

"We have some more questions for her regarding the assault that took place on a train a few days ago and the subsequent disappearance of the victim from the hospital," the officer said as he stepped back and turned his flat black eyes on Grandpa Able. "Understand that, if you interfere with our investigation, you will be prosecuted to the full extent of the law."

"Are you threatening me, son?" Grandpa Able said in a calm voice. "I served two tours in Vietnam, and you dare to threaten me." His face flushed in anger. "Get off my property before I call the department and talk to your boss. I've known Stan Thurston since he was first hired to the department. He and I play golf on weekends."

The officer glared at Grandpa Able for a few more moments, and then turned and walked back to where his cruiser was parked. Before he got into the car he turned and looked back, his voice was chilling as he called back loudly. "You think only one of your granddaughters can disappear, old man?"

Grandpa Able stared in amazement at the retreating police vehicle. How could the officer make such a blatant threat? He stumbled backwards and pushed the door shut. As he looked back out the living room window, he saw the police cruiser turn the corner and disappear down the street. Less then a minute later, Jacob's Mustang turned the same corner and drove down the street. The panic that had been about to set into his mind settled down as Jacob's Mustang pulled into the driveway.

"Oh, thank the Lord," Grandpa Able muttered when Jane and Jacob climbed out of the vehicle and both started towards the house. They were smiling and chatting like old friends, and he shook his head to clear the dark thoughts that had grown so quickly with the threat.

"What happened?" Jane asked as she climbed the porch steps and noticed the troubled look on Grandpa Able's face. She hurried up the rest of the steps and gave him a big hug, then stepped back with a worried look on her face and waited for him to respond.

"What happened to you, girl?" Grandpa Able asked, ignoring her concern and seeing noticed how dirty she was.

"Hiking got a little dirtier than we thought it would be," Jane said with a laugh. "I slipped a few times, but Jacob managed to come through the whole thing without much on him."

Jacob smiled and looked at Jane as if noticing for the first time exactly how dirty she was. He saw two rips on the right leg of her pants and patches of dried mud that had soaked into both her shirt and pants. She was filthy, maybe, but he still thought she was the prettiest girl he had ever known.

"A police officer was here just a minute ago looking for you two," Grandpa Able explained as he sat down slowly and leaned back in his chair on the porch. "I sent him packing and told him I was going to call Stan if he caused any problems."

"Grandpa, maybe they just wanted to fill us in on the whole train incident," Jane said slowly as her mind raced. They had already told their story numerous times. Why would the police be looking for her and Jacob again?

"I didn't like the look of him," Grandpa Able muttered with a frown. "I spent twelve years in the marines and did two tours in Vietnam. I am not going to be threatened by some punk kid in a uniform that doesn't fit him. Now that I think about it, he had the weirdest looking pin just above his badge. There must be something against that in the departments uniform code."

Jane and Jacob looked at each other, their faces going pale, and both thinking of what would happen if the Adherents had managed to get people hired into the police department, and how much more difficult things would be here in their world.

"Well now, you two look like you just saw the ghost of a pirate ship," Grandpa Able laughed as he shook off the irritation of the oddly dressed police officer with Jane safely home. "Come on in. Have a brownie. I just took a pan out of the oven about thirty minutes ago."

Jane smiled.

"And there might even be a bucket of ice cream in the freezer," Grandpa Able said with a smile. "Besides, you both look like you've been skipping meals lately. Come on, Jacob, have some ice cream. Football season isn't for a couple months yet." Grandpa Able stood up and led them into the house, then stopped and turned to lock the front door after they were all inside. *Not worth taking any chances with the strange happenings nowadays*, Grandpa Able thought.

"All right, you talked me into it," Jacob said with a smile. He followed Jane down the short hallway to the kitchen and dining room area. The floors in the old house were maple, and a long runner rug trailed from the front door to the arched passage into the kitchen. On the right, stairs led up to the single upstairs bedroom, and on the left a wide area opened up into a living room with a television mounted on the far wall. The tiling in the kitchen was perfectly placed and matched the carpet runner. Jacob knew Grandpa Able was proud of his kitchen. Grandma Kay sat at the kitchen table with a big book of word search puzzles. She smiled as they entered and held out her arms to Jane. Grandma Kay hugged her warmly, and the concern left her face.

"Jacob, good to see you," Grandma Kay said warmly. "Tell me you're treating our little Jany right."

"Grandma . . ." Jane said, mortified. She hated the nickname ever since she turned thirteen. Her face blushed brightly.

"Jany?" Jacob asked, grinning. His voice faltered as she turned and glared at him. "Sorry, I'll never say it again" he whispered as he hid a smile behind his hand. Thankfully Grandpa Able set down a gallon of New York vanilla on the table and an ice cream scoop.

"Grandma, do you want some?" Jane asked as she hugged her grandmother tightly once again.

"No, dearie, I'm fine," Grandma Kay replied. "Why don't you go get changed so we can get a load of laundry going with those dirty clothes."

Jane rolled her eyes but went upstairs and spent ten minutes cleaning up before she brought her clothes back down and threw them into the laundry hamper. When the ice cream was served and each bowl was topped with a brownie and finally smothered in a thick layer of chocolate syrup, they all walked over to the living room and found a place to sit.

"When will your mom be home tonight?" Grandpa Able asked Jacob as he dipped into the bowl.

"I don't know," Jacob admitted. "She works late most nights. Is that a new iPad?"

On the small coffee table was a white box emblazoned with the image of the now iconic device. It was still sealed shut, and Grandpa Able motioned to it. "Yes, I bought it last week knowing Jane would be here to show us how to operate the durn thing. We haven't had time so far though."

"Can I open it up for you?" Jacob said excitedly. "I've always wanted to play around with one of them." He picked up the box and turned it over in his hands examining it from all sides.

"Sure." Grandpa Able passed him a small knife. Everyone watched as he slit the box and slid out the styrofoam packaging. The actual case itself was black. The sticker on the side said it was a 64G model. "We're supposed to start using it to talk to my sister-in-law in Hawaii. Everyone said it was an easy way to see her while we talked. I just don't know how it works."

Jane slipped from her seat next to her grandpa and plopped down next to Jacob, leaning on his shoulder and slowly spooned the ice cream into her mouth as she watched. "Look, there's the Skype icon," she said as she pointed with her spoon and almost dripped ice cream onto the tablet. "Oops." She pulled her spoon back hastily and licked the extra ice cream from the metal.

"Here, plug it in to charge the battery," Jacob replied as he handed her the cord. He turned the iPad over and plugged in the cord on his end.

Jane plugged the cord in and then snuggled in close next to Jacob and watched as his finger flipped over the applications until they found the Skype icon. They spent the next hour setting it up. When Jane finally looked up to tell her grandpa they had it ready, she realized she and Jacob were sitting on the couch alone and the living room was otherwise empty.

"They must have gone to bed," Jane said with a smile. "We had better at least put Angry Birds and a couple other games on there just in case we get bored at some point."

Jacob laughed and then continued downloading different things until they were both yawning. "We'd better get some sleep. In the morning, Tasker's expecting us back with a good excuse to stay all day."

"Hiking again?"

"It worked last time," Jacob laughed. "Might as well stick with what works."

"Maybe fishing?" Jane suggested. "That way if we come back smelling like fish, no one will think anything of it." She wrinkled her nose at the thought of smelling like fish all day, but the last trip had made them fairly fragrant.

"Maybe, but I should leave the car somewhere down by the docks," Jacob said a little worried. He didn't want some of his rivals to see his car unattended for a any period of time. Too many pranks went on around the team.

"What about we tell them we're going hiking on the Wisconsin side," Jane said. "That'd work just as well and leave us a bit of wiggle room. And it is technically true—we will be in Wisconsin."

"Sounds fine," Jacob said as he set the iPad on the coffee table and turned to look at her. "I better get some sleep then, I suppose."

Jane sighed as he stood and walked to the door, "I'll see you tomorrow."

"Tomorrow it is," Jacob said with smile. "Make sure you relock the door after I leave." He waved to her and slipped outside. He stood on the porch until he heard the dead bolt slide home. The night was warm as he walked to his car, but he still shivered a little as he opened the door and slid into the seat. The engine roared to life, and he rolled the window down as he put the car in reverse and started backing out of the driveway. Suddenly there was a flash of police lights, and a police department squad car pulled up behind him.

"What in the world?" Jacob muttered. "How can they pull me over when I'm sitting in a driveway, not moving?" He waited as the officer approached the car, and he heard the thin voice tell him to keep his hands in plain sight.

He put both hands on the wheel and nervously twisted his thick ring around, he looked in the side mirror. He noticed the officer wore a uniform several sizes too big for him and his face reminded Jacob of the Adherents they had dealt with over the last two days. Quickly he slipped the ring from his hand and dropped it onto the seat release lever. He heard the metal slide down until it came to a halt against the seat.

"Turn the car off!"

Jacob complied. He noticed that Grandpa Able and Jane were standing on the porch next to the front door watching what was happening. He waved and smiled at them and shrugged.

"Get out and place your hands behind your head."

"What did I do?" Jacob asked as he stepped out of the car and looked at the officer with his arms above his head.

"Put your hands behind your head!"

"I haven't done anything," Jacob repeated as he complied. He was roughly shoved against the side of the car and his hands were wrenched behind his back as steel cuffs were strapped to his wrists. He shook his head. This was all wrong.

"Jane, take care of my car please," Jacob said as he was being led away. He made a point of spreading his hands behind his back and pointing at the empty place on his ring finger, hoping she would catch on. "I left the keys in it for you!" he shouted to her. He tried to turn his head to see if she was following what he was asking, but the officers shoved him into the back of the squad and told him to, "Stop shouting!"

A minute later he was in the back of the squad car watching as Jane cried and Grandpa Able argued with the officer. He couldn't hear what was being said, but the anger showed on both of their faces as did the smug look on the officer's.

* * * * *

Two weeks earlier

"TELL ME ABOUT YOUR FAMILY," Carvin asked. He was sitting with his back against the wall next to the door.

Jackie glanced over at him and lowered the fork that she had been using to eat. She noticed that over the last few weeks he had been bringing her food more and more often and she was starting to look forward to the visits.

"I have a sister," Jackie said finally. She knew she should hold her silence but she had been here for weeks and boredom was taking its toll.

"I wish I had another brother," Carvin said quietly. He rubbed his face nervously. If his father found out that he was here, he would get in terrible trouble.

"What happened to him?" Jackie asked curiously.

"My father killed him about two years ago," Carvin said. He knew he should feel more sadness over the death of his only brother but there was never much love lost between the two. "My brother refused to follow my father's orders one day and my father struck him with his fist. He fell backwards and struck his head against the wall. A day later, he died."

"How terrible," Jackie said. She was surprised to find that she actually felt sorry for him.

The conversation turned to lighter topics and Jackie actually laughed more than once. Even more importantly, she began to gain an understanding of how this world operated as related to her world.

"So you're telling me that there are two worlds side by side," Jackie repeated incredulously. "And they are separated by this Divide thing?"

"Yes," Carvin said with a nod of his head.

"But . . ." Jackie started but stopped. She was having a hard time accepting any of what he was telling her. Still, how could she argue with the fact that she was locked in a cell in a place that was obviously not on her earth?

CHAPTER TWO

Adherents Everywhere

"I AM TELLING YOU, STAN, one of your officers came here and arrested him," Grandpa Able repeated into the phone. He stopped and listened a couple minutes, then shook his head, "How can that be? The kid is a star on the football team and the nicest boy you could ever meet."

Against her will, Jane tuned out the conversation. It was nearly midnight and she was exhausted. She had retrieved the keys from Jacob's car and locked the doors, but something still rang in her mind. Why would Jacob care about his car when he was being led away in handcuffs? They had pulled the Mustang into the garage next to her grandpa's car. She walked to the side door and entered the garage, flipping on the lights and replaying the event in her mind once more. She opened the door to the Mustang and sat down in the driver's seat. It wasn't set for her so she reached down and felt around for the seat release, when she found it she pulled it up and slid the seat forward. When it was placed perfectly she released the lever and stopped. Suddenly, she thought she heard a clinking sound beneath her.

"What's down there," Jane muttered. She reached down with both hands and felt the release bar. There it was, the ring Jacob had gotten from Tasker. She breathed a sigh of relief. "Now I just have to figure out a way to get it back to him without the police suspecting anything." She knew if the police had taken Jacob they would have found the ring for sure. At least this way she stood a chance of getting it to him where they could use it without being seen. At least the ring was not on its way to Cain.

"What did Stan say?" Jane asked when she walked back into the house. The garage doors were locked but she locked the inner door as well.

"He's going down to the station to check on it, but it's going to take him a while," Grandpa Able replied. They both sat on the couch dozing until almost three in the morning when the phone rang again.

"Stan?" Grandpa Able said as he answered the phone. He listened for a while, and then finally hung up the phone and looked troubled. "He said the officers had an anonymous tip that there were drugs in the Tanner's house. They got a search warrant and found cocaine and drug paraphernalia spread out all over the basement."

"What!" Jane gasped. "No . . . !" She stopped herself before she continued. She couldn't admit she had been inside Jacob's house. Not when she had told her grandparents she was a hundred miles away hiking.

"He said they arrested his mom and Jacob," Grandpa Able said. "But he didn't think they'd hold the boy for long, just Mrs. Tanner."

"We have to go see him," Jane burst out in tears.

"I asked him that. He said he'd arrange something for first thing in the morning," Grandpa Able replied. "It was the best he could do." Grandpa Able sighed and shook his head, "We should probably try to get some sleep."

Jane just nodded numbly. How far did the Adherent's tendrils reach into their world? Where could they go to hide from them? Or was it impossible? Would Cain take out her support one piece at a time?

She stumbled upstairs and collapsed into her bed. Sleep came very slowly as Jane lay staring at the ceiling, trying to decide how to proceed. Did she go visit Tasker and explain the situation or would she try to find a way to get the ring to Jacob so he could free himself and hide out across the Divide? Finally she dropped into an exhausted slumber. Her dreams were dark and ominous.

The next morning her grandpa woke her at nine by tapping on her door. "Jany, we need to leave soon," Grandpa Able said as he tapped on the door again.

"Okay, I'm awake," Jane said sleepily. Then she bolted straight up in bed and looked around as panic set in and the memories of the night before slowly filtered back into her mind. She heard her grandpa going back downstairs. She gathered her things and slipped into the bathroom for a quick shower. After drying her hair and tying it back in a ponytail she hurried downstairs and rushed into the kitchen.

"Breakfast is set out," Grandpa Able said and pointed at the table. "As soon as you get done, we'll go over to the police station."

Jane wolfed down the food, and then put on her shoes and followed Grandpa Able out the door. They backed out of the garage and headed down the street until they reached a road that went through to the lake. Grandpa Able turned the Crown Victoria down the hill and went towards the lake until he finally linked up with London Road. Traffic was light, and they made it onto Highway 35 quickly. Jane stared out the window with Jacob's ring around her thumb. Tucked inside her sweater was her map and pen. Pinned to the outside of her sweater was her anchor. She didn't know what she was going to do, but she came prepared to do whatever was needed. Jacob had to have his ring and anchor to her map. With that he could escape the Adherents to the Divide and seek help from Tasker on the other side. Suddenly she smiled and shook her head. Did she really want help from Tasker right now? He couldn't even operate a car handle.

They exited the highway and turned onto North Lake Avenue for two blocks, then took the left into the police department parking lot. Grandpa Able slipped into a parking spot. They entered the building and spoke to an officer at the front desk who seemed to not know anything about the case, but since he knew Grandpa Able, he called Stan. A few minutes later they were sitting in the chief's office.

"They found a substantial amount of illegal drugs inside the residence," Stan said in a tired voice. "I've spoken to the officers involved because most of them are new to the force, but they seemed to have followed the proper procedures. Several other officers I trust implicitly were with them when they entered the house."

"This isn't right," Jane insisted. "We were out hiking all day yesterday, and we were at the beach the day before. I talked to his mom. She showed me around the house the first day. There was nothing. Now you make it sound like the drugs were scattered everywhere." She burst into tears when she was done and buried her face in her hands. "If they were all around the house, I would have seen something."

"I know that boy, Stan," Grandpa Able muttered. "He isn't the type."

Stan stood and walked to the door. He closed it and lowered the shade on his window, "Look, Able, I agree with you. There's something fishy going on here, but I can't seem to lay my hand on what it is yet.

These officers were hired just before I became chief, and the old chief had some strange ideas now and then. Just last year I had to send him to St. Peter. His family had him committed. He kept rambling on about people disappearing and strange lights in the skies. Thing is, these new guys haven't done anything to warrant my firing them."

Jane's tears slowed as she listened to him.

"I have watched Jacob grow up, and I've known his mother for fifteen years," Stan muttered quietly. "Neither one of them is into drugs. That much I know for a fact."

"But then ..." Jane started to say.

"I had to hold them both at least for the night," Stan admitted. "Someone alerted the newspapers, and we've had reporters all over town because of these freak waves. Now I have people from the drug enforcement agency calling and demanding custody, quoting some law or federal regulation I can't even find on their website. The feds say if I don't turn them over to them, they'll come after me and the department."

"But—" Jane started again, and again Stan cut her off.

"I won't let them take Jacob," Stan said. "That one I can fight because he's underage, but I can do little for his mom if they have the proper paperwork. I can probably delay them a day or two, but that's it."

Jane's mind swirled around, wondering what to do. "Can we talk to them?"

Stan frowned, but finally he nodded, "I'll arrange something. You'll have to leave your phones and electronic devices here in my office."

They waited while he picked up the phone and made a few calls. Then he led them down to the main floor of the station and into a stark interview room. A metal table against one wall was bolted to the floor. Two plastic chairs sat near the table, and a brilliant fluorescent light added just the right amount of sterile light to the area. They stood waiting for nearly twenty minutes before an officer walked Jacob into the room and motioned for him to sit down.

"Jacob!" Jane burst out as she threw her arms around him and hugged him tightly. When she finally let go of him, they separated slowly and looked around as if remembering for the first time that others were present.

"Sir," Jacob started out as soon as he sat back down. "I didn't do anything. I wasn't even home yesterday."

"I know, son," Stan replied as he raised his hands helplessly. "But I have a signed search warrant from Judge Thompson and supply of drugs that matches the packaging and types of items similar to what we took off a dealer less than a week ago." Suddenly he stopped and listened to his radio for a minute. "Blast it, the federal officers are here already." He stepped out of the room and closed the door, leaving them alone.

"What's going on?" Jacob asked. "I sat in a holding cell by myself all night with the lights on, trying to figure out what was happening."

"I don't know," Grandpa Able said. "They claim they found drugs in your house that match something they found earlier this week."

"I never!"

"I know, son, and so does the chief, so he's trying to delay the federal officers right now," Grandpa Able explained.

Suddenly the door swung open, and Stan stepped back into the room followed by two thin men in dark suits. Jane's eyes saw the anchors pinned to their chests immediately, and she knew by the intake of breath next to her that Jacob did also. Two more local officers entered the hearing room right after the agents. All of a sudden the interview room was very crowded.

"We'll take him with us," the first agent said with a grim smile. "We know how to deal with his type."

"Not so fast. Jacob isn't going anywhere considering he's only sixteen," Stan replied. "I have some paperwork I need filled out and few things I need to check on first. Officers Lee and Marks will make sure everyone stays put until I give the word for you to leave."

"You can't stop . . ." one of the men started but he stopped as Stan took a step closer and glared at him.

"This is my department, and I run it," Stan growled. "Not you. Get that straight." The two men scowled at each other for what seemed like five minutes before the federal agent stepped back and nodded.

The two local officers took up a position on either side of the door.

"I'll be back in a few minutes. Able, can you come with me? We have a few things to talk about," Stan said and then he stepped back out of the room. Grandpa Able followed him. Suddenly Jane felt very alone despite the presence of so many people still in the room. The moment the door closed, the thin man turned and smiled at them.

"He can't stop us," the second man stated to Jacob as though everyone else was invisible. "We can take you out any time we want to. You think your family's safe? Do you think anyone you love is safe? We can reach out to you anywhere you hide."

"Adherent!" Jacob hissed, and he was rewarded with a slightly surprised look on the federal agents' faces. "I know that's who you are."

"Give us the ring, and we'll make this go away," the first man replied.

Jane stared at the man with an open mouth. That was what they wanted, the Runners Ring. She bit down on her lip and slipped her hands into her pocket and ran a finger over the metal loop.

"Well, I don't have it now, do I?" Jacob said as he held up his empty fingers and wiggled them in the man's face. He glanced over at the two uniformed officers and noticed they were watching closely but neither seemed likely to interfere unless they absolutely had to.

"Great thing about this world boy," Cain's runner said with a smile. "The technology they have can be used for so many things. It's too bad that much of it doesn't survive the trip back through the Divide." Suddenly the man pulled a stun gun from his belt. In one fluid motion he aimed it at the officer standing to the left of the door.

Jacob saw his eyes widen as the metal prongs struck his chest. Then the Adherent triggered the device, and the police officer collapsed to the floor as his body jerked wildly.

"What the . . . !" The second officer reached for his gun, but a second set of prongs struck him in the shoulder. He fell to the floor.

Jane lunged toward Jacob and pulled the ring from her pocket. She threw the metal band and anchor at him, and then crashed into the Adherents. The man stumbled backwards. Then Jane activated her own anchor. The room around her disappeared. Her own map was tucked tightly inside her windbreaker along with the compass and pen. Her anchor was fastened to the inside of her jacket out of sight. Before leaving home she had hurriedly found the place on her map where she wished to exit, and suddenly the wooden walls of the fort on Stockton Island appeared.

CHAPTER THREE

Lost Tribes

TASKER HURRIED BACK to the small command post when the goblin appeared nearby and told him one of his humans had arrived. When he stepped into the building, he found a worried Jane looking about wildly. She seemed to have just stepped from the Divide and looked scared.

"Where's Jacob?" Tasker asked as he looked about for the boy.

"I don't know. He should be close behind me," Jane said breathlessly. "We ran into some trouble." She ran outside.

Suddenly Jacob appeared. "They shot me," Jacob muttered in surprise. He looked over at them, then down at his stomach where a spreading stain of red had appeared. His hands clutched at the wound, and then he collapsed to the ground with a groan.

"Jacob!" Jane screamed. She bolted to his side and carefully rolled him to his back. There was a puncture wound in the side of his stomach and a steady stream of blood seeped out of the small hole. The bullet must have passed completely through because there was a bigger wound on his lower back where the blood also flowed freely.

"Quickly! Carry him inside!" Tasker shouted at a pair of sailors standing nearby staring wide eyed. They hurried over and gently picked up Jacob as Jane kept his hands pressed firmly to the wounds. They hustled through the front door and laid him gently on the table while Tasker rinsed his hands in clean water and then hurried over. He leaned close and examined the wounds while Jane clung to Jacob's hand.

"This is bad," Tasker said finally, leaning back. He leaned as close to the wound as he could and sniffed deeply.

"It can't be that bad," Jane sobbed. "It looks like the bullet went right through. Won't it heal?" She was shaking, and tears rolled down her face.

"It isn't the wound. That we can heal," Tasker muttered. "They dipped the projectile in poison, even the slightest contact with the blood and the venom begins to work."

"There must be something we can do?" Jane said as she wiped her tears away.

Jacob groaned where he lay on the table, and a cold sweat broke out across his face. She helped Tasker cleanse the wound. They tore long sections from a clean cloth and folded them over until two thick bandages sat on the table.

"Put this under him," Tasker muttered. He removed a clay flask from a nearby shelf and poured a bit of a foul-smelling liquid across the cloth. Carefully he placed the treated bandage under the exit wound and poured the same amount of liquid on the bandage for the second wound. He motioned Jane to hold the thick bandage in place while he carefully slid a long cloth under Jacob's body and wrapped it around twice. When he had pulled it snug, he tied it together and stepped back.

"What do we do?" Jane asked again. Her tears had run their course, and she stood stoically waiting for Tasker to answer her. "Do I take him back to my world and find a hospital?"

"No!" Tasker replied immediately. "He won't last that long, besides the poison is native to this world. Nothing that works in your world would have any effect on a poison from this side of the Divide."

"What kind of poison is it?" Jane asked.

"It's made from the leaves of the Bausor tree," Tasker muttered. "Very rare and shipped from very far away."

"So what do we do?" Jane insisted. Her face pale as she pleaded for some way to cure Jacob. "There must be some way to cure it."

"I treated the bandage with a potion that'll slow the spread of the poison but it won't stop it," Tasker explained. "We have maybe a day at most to find a cure, and our best efforts should go towards finding the People of the Wood."

"Who are they?" Jane asked as she gently ran her finger along Jacob's fevered brow. His face was hot, and droplets of sweat formed on his skin. They slowly came together and slipped down the table, where they formed a pool on the wood.

"They came from your world when the Divide was put in place," Tasker explained. He unrolled his map on the bunk nearby and pointed to an area of land that was blank except for one word. "The Lost Ojibwa, they are called in your world, and their lands once surrounded the Black Leech Lake. The people who live there are firm believers in the great spirits, and they were deemed to be a better fit for our world than yours. They were one of the first peoples that Cain turned his sights against when he gained power here and he hurt them horribly. However, some hidden communities survived. We need to find one of them and gain the aid of their shaman. In fact, I know of one who has the knowledge and power to banish this type of poison from the veins . . . that is if he survived the purges."

"Where can we find them now?" Jane asked.

"Those who survived retreated deep into the remains of the great underground dwarf mines dug many centuries ago. Cain let them be because he believed he had sealed all ways of entering or exiting the mines, but this isn't true. I found a single entrance while searching for signs proving that the Lost Ojibwa had survived. At the entrance the eagle of the great band had been etched into the stone, and I knew at least one of their medicine men had survived."

"Where?" Jane insisted. "And when can we leave?"

"We'll leave immediately," Tasker replied. "I'll tell you exactly where when we arrive."

Jane leaned over Jacob and touched his fevered forehead one last time. He seemed to be sleeping, but his breath was shallow, and his eyes seemed to be moving rapidly behind the closed lids.

"Keep him here, Bella, and keep him safe," Tasker instructed the fairy. "Use your magic to keep him from moving. Movement will only spread the poison more rapidly."

Bella fluttered over to Jacob, and, started over his feet, slowly built a glowing net around his body. His troubled sleep quieted. "It works better each time you use it on someone," Bella explained when she fluttered back over to where they were standing. "If there were more fairies here, we could strengthen the net and keep him perfectly still. There's strength in numbers where fairy magic is concerned."

"Keep him safe for me," Jane said with a teary smile. She turned and followed Tasker out the door and looked around the fort. It was obvious that the dwarf and his force of rebels had been busy. Even though she had only been away a little more than a day, the walls had been repaired, and the two giants and three trolls were busy hauling timbers from the forest and dropping them near the outer gates. Half a dozen men with axes limbed the trees, and two more with a rough two-sided saw hacked the logs into long sections to be added to the walls.

"Puck has been at work on a mushroom ring here on Stockton Island," Tasker explained as he led her down the rough dirt road and to the edge of the forest. "They only grow in the wild, so we need to walk into the forest aways."

Jane thought they walked for almost two-hundred yards before the forest opened up, and they found Eriunia and Puck leaning over a circle of mushrooms in the meadow. The tall willowy elf had replace her tattered clothes with a sturdy pair of trousers and a tunic that offered her more modesty than her old prisoner clothes. Her hair was pulled back into a pony tail similar to Jane's, and she smiled brilliantly when she saw Jane.

"Welcome back," Eriunia said and hugged Jane warmly. "I think the ring is ready."

"Good," Tasker muttered gruffly. "Jacob was poisoned by an Adherent. If we don't find a cure quickly he won't survive."

Jane glanced at the dwarf and wondered at the directness suddenly in his voice. She was more used to Tasker beating around what he was trying to say, but with all watchers gone, he seemed to lower his defenses and admit that things were grave.

"What will you do?"

"The poison is from a Bausor tree," Tasker explained. "What would you do?"

The elf's hand went to her mouth and shock showed in her eyes.

"Very rare," Puck mumbled. "And very expensive. Only a few places can you find anyone who'll harvest the Bausor tree, let alone find someone who will transport it half way around the world."

"I'm well aware of the difficulty of finding the poison itself," Tasker said. "I'm seeking a cure, one that can be had quickly."

"If the way weren't closed to Tuatha De Danaan, there's skill and mystic knowledge there to heal such a poison, but here in the mortal realm . . ." Eriunia shook her head. "What here has the power to heal such a thing?"

"There's someone nearby who has the skill and knowledge," Tasker muttered. "Someone Cain believes to be dead, but finding him won't easy. I'll need your help, Eriunia, if you'll agree." They all waited for Tasker to continue. "There were those native to this land of forests before the Divide was put in place. There's a shaman among the ranks of those who came to this side of the Divide who can help us."

"You're speaking of the Lost Ojibwa," Puck muttered. "My goblins have searched the forests for many years and have seen no signs of their survival. What makes you think you can find them?"

"You were searching the wrong places," Tasker said. "Puck, please keep our forces together and ready the ships. Eriunia, Jane, and myself will go searching for Walks with Clouds, the last shaman of the Lost Ojibwa. He alone is close enough for us to seek his help. When we return, it'll be with his aid or not at all. Without Jacob's aid, the battle for Madeline Island will be much bloodier then it needs to be."

"I'll do what I can," Puck replied. He seemed unnaturally quiet and somber as he walked back into the woods and in the direction of the fort.

"We are going to come out in the mushroom ring alongside Serpent Lake," Tasker said as they looked down at the mushroom circle. "It's called Serpent Lake for a reason. Whatever you do, stick close to me. We'll head north to the Ports Mouth Mine where my ancestors opened up the first tunnels to the surface so many thousands of years ago."

"Snakes," Jane muttered as her face paled. "I hate snakes." They all stepped into the mushroom circle and were soon flashing along the magical passages under Tasker's direction.

It took a few minutes of travel. When they finally stepped out of the flashing circle Jane looked around nervously, hoping no snakes were close by. It was mid-morning, and the sun reflected off the surface of the water about two-hundred feet from where a small circle of oak trees watched over the mushroom circle. Suddenly Jane saw a ripple pass across the surface of the water. Moments later it seemed like the water boiled upwards. Then a massive head broke the surface and rose high into the air and looked down at them with glittering eyes. What made her heart pound even faster was that the gigantic snake's body was topped with a human looking head and a mouth wide open and full of long fangs. She stared at the creature in amazement as it moved slowly towards the shore and hissed loudly at them.

"Now is a good time to run," Tasker said. He grabbed both of the women by the arms and pulled them away from the lake.

Jane didn't need to be told a second time. She turned and bolted away, running as fast her long legs would carry and glancing over her shoulder once or twice to check if the great creature was chasing them. Eriunia matched her stride for stride, and soon it was Tasker who was frantically pumping his legs as he tried to catch up with the other two.

"What in the world was that?" Jane gasped when she finally stopped running and the dwarf managed to catch them.

"That was a Naga, more common in places like distant India, but they found ways to spread even here to the new world. Many snake creatures were forced into our world after the Divide was raised," Tasker said as he panted for breath. "Despite being a common-place animal, serpents of such size are too central to the greatest legends and were deemed magical and, therefore, subject to the ban. I didn't know a Naga had made the trip here, however. This may complicate our efforts to return to Stockton Island."

"Do you think!" Jane shouted. She looked nervously back towards the lake. "I'm not going anywhere near that thing again." Then she paused and looked around. "How do we know it isn't chasing us?"

"That particular creature doesn't like dry land," Tasker said. "I'm surprised he left the water at all." He rose to his feet and motioned for them to follow him. "The place we seek isn't far. I found it many years ago when I first . . ." he paused. "Well, when I was exploring the new world." He glanced at Jane but found her more interested in watching the forest around them then noticing his near slip.

They walked north through the thick forest until the trees suddenly opened up and Jane found herself standing on the edge of a deep pit cut into the ground. Around the edge of the pit were the remains of ancient stone stairs. They circled the outside and led down into the gloom that filled the bottom of the pit.

"Where are we?" Jane asked. She knew her map didn't extend this far, and the thought of being stranded far from any way of escape did not make her feel any better.

"In your world it's called the Portsmouth Mine. It filled with water and was left," Tasker explained as he stepped onto the first of the ancient stone steps. "In this world the pit was opened by a race of ancient dwarves who emerged from the ground soon after the Divide was created. They lived hidden from both sides until then. When they felt the power of the Divide sunder their world, they came to find out what had happened. Many of their people were stranded on each side of the Divide, and they never forgave the Seely Court for its decision."

Jane followed Tasker down the steps. "What's this Seely Court I've heard you mention?" She stopped for a minute. Then another thought hit her, "Are you telling me some of the dwarves still exist in my world?"

"We're not sure if they still survive," Tasker admitted. "There are places people on your side of the Divide haven't explored under the surface of the world, and my people are experts at remaining hidden underground." He paused before answering her other question. "As for the court, it's a gathering of representatives from the most powerful races," Tasker explained. "They're the guiding force behind the committees and provide direction on issues that affect all the mythical and magical races."

"They're a bunch of busy bodies who should mind their own business," Eriunia muttered from behind Jane. "They're part of the reason the elvish race cut itself off from the worlds."

An uncomfortable silence descended on the trio as they followed the edges of the irregular pit down into the ground. Around them the walls were damp and covered with moss, and the sickly sweet smell of rotting leaves and mold filled the air. Jane sneezed several times as she fought against urges to flee. The light faded until they were walking down into the ground in what seemed like the half-light of sunset. Jane looked up when they reached the bottom and decided they must be at least a hundred and fifty yards underground. The bottom of the pit opened up around them. Pools of stagnant water filled the dips in the ground. Tasker led them across the stone until they reached the side of the pit.

"There it is," Tasker said slowly. He pointed at the symbol painted above the door, the image of the eagle surrounded the triangle shape and was painted in black with his wings outstretched as though protecting the stone door set into the side of the mine.

"Why would they retreat underground?" Jane asked. She had read some of the histories of what the Native American peoples had faced in her own world and wondered if it was at all similar.

"I don't know the entire story," Tasker replied. "I know Cain tried to contact them, and soon after horrible plagues broke out across their lands. Those who survived were hunted by Cain's Adherents and were forced to flee. The last contact I had with Walks with Clouds was . . ." he paused for a moment. "Well, it was a long time ago."

"How do we enter?" Jane asked. She put her hand against the stone and felt the rough surface, it was gritty and almost wet under her fingers but her thoughts kept returning to Jacob and his desperate plight.

"I don't know," Tasker admitted as he examined the stone portal. "This was as close as I was able to make it."

CHAPTER FOUR

Dream Catchers

SILENCE DESCENDED in the musty pit as Tasker and Eriunia stood before the closed stone gate and examined the eagle painted above the mantel. Jane stepped back ten feet and looked up at the whole scene and tried to find anything she thought looked out of place or different.

"Couldn't I draw a map of the pit and step behind the door?" Jane asked suddenly.

"If you were a runner, yes," Tasker replied. "A good runner has that much control, but I don't think it would be wise for a map maker to attempt it."

"Can I erase the door for a minute, and we step through it?" Jane questioned. "Like I did with the tunnel at the Prison Islands?"

"It's hand made," Tasker pointed out. "If it was natural, yes, but with it being hand crafted, it's immune to alteration by a map maker. It'd resist any attempt to remove it even for a moment of time. Remember, if I'm correct, this door was put in place to protect the Lost Ojibwa from Cain and his Adherents. They wouldn't make it easy for anyone to enter."

They examined the door, and Jane chaffed at the delay, every moment they stood trying to gain entrance to the underground mine was a moment closer to Jacob's death. She couldn't take the pressure. "We should have brought Jacob's sword with us," Jane muttered. "We could have cut the dang thing out."

"Wait a minute," Eriunia said suddenly as she leaned forward and examined the painting above the door. She reached up and touched the spot where the eagle's single eye looked down at them. "Look, the eye isn't just painted, it's carved into the stone. The same thing is true where its heart should be. Look around the bottom of the pit. I'm willing to bet there are similar carvings somewhere else with parts that can be removed and placed into these spots." She pointed to the two places and then began to poke around the floor excitedly.

31

Jane looked around, taking stock of the bottom of the pit. The area was less than a hundred feet across, and it had been mined into a narrow oval shape. From where she stood, she could see a number of pools and a couple of places where the stones of the floor had lifted up. Other than those features, the ground was flat. The walls around them were rugged but she could not see anything that looked out of place. Slowly she walked around until she was completely across the floor from Tasker and Eriunia but still could not find anything.

"I can't see anything," Jane called across the bottom of the pit. She looked around once more, and then thought about how the bottom of the pit looked vaguely familiar. Then her heart started to beat faster. She vaulted up a dozen steps until she could see the entire pit floor through the gloom. "Now I see it," she laughed. She pointed down at the ground before her. "It's the pools of water carved into the floor."

Sure enough. Barely visible in the dim light, the pools of water matched the carved eagle above the door perfectly. She hurried back down to the floor and walked to where a small mound of stone marked the place where the eagle's eye was located. They all gathered around and examined the stone. Eriunia suddenly pointed at a crevasse in the rock craftily hidden under a shadowy ridge in the stone.

Jane slipped her hand up and over the edge of the stone and felt around under the lip of the rock until her fingers found a round stone that came free in her hand. She smiled and pulled it out and found that she was holding a perfectly round stone that held the lines of a Lake Superior agate. The stone was brilliant red and muted brown with thousands of tiny lines that wove across the surface, forming what looked eerily like an eye that seemed to be staring at her. She walked across the pit floor and slipped the eye into place. The moment it touched the painted eagle, the painted lines shimmered for a moment and stopped as the eye rotated slowly and looked at them.

"Quick we need the heart too," Jane cried. She ran to where the triangle pool of water was carved into the floor. The water was stagnant and brackish and the rocks at the edge of the small pool of water were covered with moss and algae. "Ick," Jane muttered as she rolled her sleeve up and dipped her hand into the water. Oddly the water was cool. She felt around the bottom of the pool until her hand suddenly came in contact with the sharp edges of a stone.

"I think I found it," Jane exclaimed. She tried to grasp it and pick it up, but the stone refused to budge. "It seems to be stuck," she muttered in frustration. With a shake of her head she pushed up her other sleeve and dipped both hands into the water. Grasping the triangle stone in both hands, she pulled against it again. Suddenly it moved, but not in the way she thought it would. Instead of coming loose from the floor, it turned in a circular manner and suddenly a grating sound filled the bottom of the mine pit. She turned and looked at the stone door in anticipation, but, oddly, the door remained firmly closed. Instead the grating sound seemed to emanate from the ground around her. Then the water in the largest pools drained away, and a series of steps began to lower slowly into the ground until the eagle shaped pools of water had formed into a passage that led even deeper underground.

"You did it, girl," Tasker said with a smile. He turned away from where he had been standing before the obviously fake door and walked to the head of the steps and peered down into the darkness. He rummaged around in his pockets for a few moments and pulled out a round wrapped package from an inner pocket. When he had completely pulled the leather wrapping off the stone, Jane saw it was a perfectly round white stone that glowed with a power that rivaled the brightest of flashlights.

"What is it?" Jane asked as she stepped closer and looked down at the round stone. Then she realized it was carved into the shape of a small round skull, and images of the last Indiana Jones movie leapt into her mind. "Hey, I've seen those before," Jane exclaimed. She looked at Tasker as he raised an eyebrow questioningly. "I saw them in a museum . . ." she paused as he continued to stare at her. "Like where they stored the maps when I saw you at the Science Museum."

"Ah," Tasker said as he nodded. "Do the ones on your side glow?"

"No," Jane replied. "In fact, the news clippings I read on them said that they were all fakes. The museum tags said they were made sometime in the last fifty years in Germany."

"I highly doubt that," Tasker said with a laugh. "Oh, I'm sure they were made in the Germanic States, but not in the last fifty years. It has been thousands of years since the Divide was put in place." Tasker paused for a moment. "Maybe there's more interest in the mythical in your world then I thought." He shook his head as he held the small crystal high and started down the steps.

"How does it glow?" Jane asked.

"It pulls its power from the magnetic lines around the world," Tasker explained. "The lines activate the power in the crystal, and they glow brightly. I bought mine in the market at Oberstein. They have a nice selection. A local band of gypsies carves them from crystal imported from one of the islands south of the Dark Continent."

The tunnel leading down into the mine was dark. For a while the passage showed signs of being carved through the stone by hands and not by nature. Bits of chisels had been discarded near the walls where they had broken, and they saw cracked wooden handles. Jane even noticed a complete hammer leaning against the wall as though waiting for some unknown hand to return and wield it.

"They left things behind when they emerged, things not being used as weapons," Tasker muttered when Jane asked him about the abandoned tools. "My ancestors were always spoiling for a fight, and they were disappointed when they failed to find one on the surface."

"So are you telling me dwarves still hide on the other side of the Divide?" Jane asked suddenly. Her voice sounded odd in the underground cavern.

"Oh, I'm sure," Tasker replied. "The Divide was a little more inconsistent as the power went underground."

"How come no one's ever seen them?" Jane persisted as she ducked under a low-hanging section of the tunnel and stepped over a pool of water."

"Many of them live deep in the world's crust," Tasker replied as he stopped at an intersection of two tunnels and examined them both. "Below even where the humans deepest mines have managed to penetrate."

"I thought the deeper you went the hotter it got," Jane asked.

"For a while," Tasker agreed. "The heat barrier was put in place to keep humans from venturing too deeply into the crust. There are other reasons, but I cannot speak of them at this time."

"Why not?" Jane asked immediately.

"Because it is not for you to know," Tasker repeated with a note of irritation.

"Why not?" Jane stated again. This time Eriunia giggled at the expression that filled Tasker's face.

"It's forbidden. That's why," Tasker growled. "Jane, there are some-things that have to be taken on faith. There are higher powers at work. I can't prove it with science but I know it is true."

Jane eyed the back of the dwarf and stuck her tongue out at him, making a face that made Eriunia snicker again. They were walking along a tunnel that angled steeply into the ground. Suddenly Tasker came to a halt as the passage stopped and a deep shaft opened up before them.

"What do we do now?" Jane asked as she leaned out over the hole and tried to see the bottom lost in the darkness.

"We climb down," Tasker said. He leaned over the edge and pointed to a series of iron stakes driven into the wall pit.

"What!" Jane exclaimed as she examined the iron spikes. "I can't climb down that."

"Then Jacob will die, and you'll be stuck here wondering if you can ever escape," Tasker said as he slipped over the edge and carefully put his feet on the nearest steps. The spikes stuck out from the wall almost a foot and provided a slightly flat place for their feet to get a grip.

"It isn't worth arguing with him," Eriunia said as she patted Jane's shoulder. "That, and I'm not sure if the passage up top is still open." Carefully the elf wormed her own body over the edge of the mine and started down behind the dwarf. "Besides . . ." she popped her head back over the top. "He has the only light."

Jane looked around as the darkness began to fill in around her and made her mind up immediately. She carefully sat down on the edge of the pit and placed her feet on the first two anchors. Slowly she turned around and let her weight rest on the spikes, she was happy to find that they held, so she slipped over the edge and began working her way from handhold to handhold. They continued down until Jane thought her arms would fail her and she'd fall, when suddenly the light became stronger, and she realized she was standing on the rocky floor of the mine pit next to Tasker. Two passages led off from the room that opened up at the bottom of the pit. Tasker examined them both before pointing to one of them.

"I think that way is our best chance," he said.

"They both look the same to me," Jane replied as she examined the passage he had not picked. In her current mood, she didn't feel like making life any easier for the dwarf.

"Yes, but this side is marked with a dream catcher," Tasker pointed to the ceiling above the passage to where a circular dream catcher was fastened to the ceiling. Four big feathers hung down to eye level. The middle of the circle was filled with a spider web of strands of some material they didn't recognize. The feathers seemed similar to eagle feathers.

"All right, I see it," Jane said as she yawned greatly. For some reason she felt the sudden urge to sleep, and she rubbed her eyes against the urges. "Wow, I didn't realize I was so tired."

Tasker took a step towards the marked passage and tried to hold his light high in the air, but his arms sagged in exhaustion. Jane tried to follow him but found her way was blocked by the sleeping form of Eriunia, who lay on the ground. Light snores issued from her lips.

"Maybe we could rest for a moment," Tasker muttered as he slumped to the ground and rested his head on his arms. His breathing steadied. A moment later he fell into a deep sleep.

Jane caught her balance and looked around as a bit of adrenaline pumped into her system. She fought against the urge to sleep. She looked up again at the dream catcher and suddenly her blood froze and her heart beat wildly, banishing all thoughts of sleep and making a cold sweat break out across her forehead. In her mind she could hear the voice of one of her friends Tara Goodwing whose father was Ojibwa.

"Dream catchers filter the bad dreams out and let the good dreams in through the feathers."

From the ceiling of the cavern hazy bits of light floated down and entered the web inside the dream catcher's circle. Jane found just by looking at them she could tell some were happy thoughts and glowed merrily as they entered the web. Others were dark floating bits of evil dreams and nightmares that joined the others entering the catcher, but this catcher was letting only the dark dreams through. Tasker groaned, and a nerve rattling shriek came from Eriunia. Both of them thrashed about in their sleep as though trying to escape the darkness that was chasing them.

Jane tried to reach up and grab the dream catcher, but it was hung too high for her to reach, and her fingers grew cold as they approached the hoop. She pulled her hand back, as feelings of fear and terror emanated from the dream catcher and made it impossible for her to even try to touch it. Suddenly she had the feeling of something watching her, and the hair on the back of her neck stood on end. She looked around and noticed for the first time a bit of light approaching from the distant depths of the passage. As she watched the approaching light, suddenly two more materialized, and Jane was forced to scramble back into the passage behind her where she clung to the wall out of sight and waited.

A few minutes later several men walked into the light of the mine entrance room and leaned over to examine the sleeping forms. Five entered the chamber, three of them carrying torches that seemed to give off no smoke at all. Jane listened as they spoke in a language she didn't understand. One of them stopped below the mine pit and held his torch high to examine the iron rungs leading up. They were all dressed in tattered buckskin leggings and vests with many beads attached to the fronts and sides. Most had feathers woven into their hair, and they bore a close resemblance to Tara Goodwing's father. Their skin was darker then Jane's, and their hair and eyes were dark, reminding her of pictures she had seen in Tara's house when she was visiting. Her friend had photos taken many years ago of Mr. Goodwing's great-grandfather, and they had taken much of the afternoon searching through boxes of the old pictures.

Jane pulled her mind back to the present and watched as two of the men hoisted the sleeping figures of Tasker and Eriunia to their shoulders. Carefully she slipped from her hiding place as the torches began to fade from view and followed the retreating figures down the cavern, wondering how she was going to free them and find a way to cure Jacob.

CHAPTER FIVE

Flying Cloud

BELLA FLUTTERED OVER the sleeping figure of Jacob nervously as her net kept him in a deep sleep that should have helped his body to heal. Instead the poison still spread slowly, and she could see the tips of his fingers beginning to turn a sickly shade of green as the poison worked its way through his blood.

"How is he?" Puck asked when he entered the room.

"Not good," Bella replied. Tasker and the others had only been gone a little more than an hour, and already rumors were traveling around the camp that the Runner was dying, and the Map maker had fled. Morale was sinking, and Puck spent the last hour trying to bolster spirits as some of the freed slaves took their families and vanished into the forests.

"I'm prepping some of the ships for battle, but if we're forced to fight against the fleet at Madeline Island with these wooden boats, it'll be a quick battle," Puck muttered.

Suddenly a flurry of shouts and calls came from outside the building, and Puck rushed to the door, his hooved feet clattered loudly on the stone floor. He threw the door open and looked out to where a trio of his goblins and two of the freed humans were leading an Adherent in a black robe towards him.

"We found him walking up the road to the fort."

Puck nodded to the goblin and looked at the Adherent. The man was short and a bit overweight, but with arms that bulged thickly under the sleeves of his robe. No anchor was attached to him anywhere. That was a good sign for the leader of the goblins. Of course there were a few runners even in Cain's service. Puck believed most of them would be kept far away from the fort until the Adherents realized what was happening. Cain was much more interested in his other activities to pull valuable resources from those to deal with a minor issue here.

"What do you want," Puck growled as his eyes flashed.

"I'm here to give you the chance to surrender," the Adherent replied evenly. "You can't possibly think you can stop the troops at the Madeline

Castle. I can promise you that, if you do not lay down your weapons by tonight, everything on this island will be burned to the ground. The commander of the Seventh Brigade has promised to be lenient to anyone who surrenders. Those who fight will be chained in cold iron and sent north to the mines."

"And if we surrender?" Puck asked curiously. Not because he had any real thoughts of stopping this fight but because he wanted to know what was on the table.

"He's promised to double the prisoner's rations and to reduce the amount of work required."

There was a round of interested muttering from some of the gathered former slaves, but many more jeers that were directed at the Adherent. "You think just because you overcame a few garrisons of guards you can beat a fully trained brigade of troops backed up by Ironships and a magic cannon?" the Adherent shouted suddenly. "Dream on. Commander Darkback has extended this offer for this one day only. Then he will land his forces and wipe this island clean. Remember, tomorrow night is full moon." The Adherent smiled as he turned and walked from the gates and under the watchful eyes of the three goblins.

"Full moon," Bella whispered in fear. "What will we do?" The legends of Commander Darkback filled the north lakes area. He was a man and a wolf, called werewolf in the legends. An exile from the old world because of his violent nature, he was a force feared by all but the most powerful of those alive today.

Puck shook his head. If Commander Darkback landed his troops and Tasker had not returned, he would abandon those he had brought here and retreat back to his woods and dream of revenge another day. Suddenly his attention was drawn to the lookout tower high above the fort. Then he heard the frantic shouts of the keen-eyed goblin stationed atop the structure.

"Ironships to the south," the goblin cried down.

"Are they approaching?" Puck called back.

"No, they seem to have dropped anchor," came the reply.

"Let me know when they start moving again!" Puck shouted back. He turned to the wood crews who were placing timbers against the inner walls. "Better make it thicker on the lake sides." Until recently, cannons had been unknown in this world. Those living here had been happy with the old ways. That all changed when the Temple of Adherence started its march across the world. Puck shook his head. Now factories and foundries dotted the countrysides, as creatures and mortals banded together for defense and struggled to build weapons to fend off invasions by other groups. How he wished to go back to the days when all he had to worry about was how to pull off his next prank and who it'd be aimed at.

"What will we do?" Bella asked again.

"Prepare for Tasker's return, and if he doesn't come in time," Puck muttered. "You and I will run for all we're worth and hope no one follows us."

Bella's tiny hand flew to her mouth as she hid a gasp. At a loss for words, she watched as Puck wandered away to watch the timbers being placed inside the wall. Then she turned back into the building where Jacob was hanging onto his life.

* * * * *

JANE FOLLOWED THE FIVE MEN of the Lost Ojibwa as they walked down the tunnel carrying the sleeping Tasker and Eriunia. The tunnel finally opened up, and she ducked behind a rock outcropping as light filled the cavern before her. When her vision cleared, she gasped openly at the sheer size of the cavern, even more impressive was the gigantic crystal that pushed out of the ground on the furthest side and glowed brilliantly, filling the area with light. It was warm and a steady push of air filled the tunnel entrance around her hiding place ruffling her hair and bringing the scent of wood smoke to her nose. About half way across the cavern a series of hide covered wigwams were clustered together behind a hill and shaded from the glowing crystal.

Around the sides of the cavern were fields filled with what looked like cornstalks and yellow hanging squash. A river flowed out from a dark hole in the wall far to her left and cut the cavern in half before disappearing out the far side into an equally dark passage. A single foot bridge stretched across the river, and Jane could see a number of figures standing along the shore throwing nets into the water and hauling them back in.

A few stands of stunted trees grew along the walls, and little channels had been dug in most places to bring water to the fields and trees.

She drew her attention back to the men carrying Tasker and Eriunia. A flurry of activity in the camp marked their arrival. Then they disappeared into a long structure covered in dirt. Since there was little cover beyond the cavern entrance, Jane slipped into a small grove of trees and examined the area. She had to do something, but just what she couldn't decide.

"Who are you?"

Jane jumped at the voice behind her and whirled around as her heart thumped wildly. Standing less than ten feet away was a girl about her own age, her skin was dark and her jet black hair was drawn back into a long braid. She wore a buckskin dress frayed at the edges but clean and sewn with many beads. A rough hoe in her hands indicated she had obviously been working on the irrigation channels when she stumbled across Jane's hiding place.

"Please, I just need my friends back," Jane stammered as she scrambled for words.

"You mean the little one and the elf?"

"Yes," Jane replied.

The native girl motioned to where the village lay further out in the cavern, "My father and the other warriors took them to the earth lodge to be seen by the elders. Outsiders are not welcome by my people since the Great Betrayal." Her copper bracelets jingled as she leaned over the small water channel and used her hoe to clear a caved-in section. Around her neck hung a thick strand of beads, and a ready smile filled her face when she looked up.

"But I'm tired of never seeing anyone but those who live in my band. What's your name?" she asked as she set the hoe down and sat on the ground with her legs folded neatly under her but off to the side.

"Jane," she replied. "What's yours?"

"Flying Cloud," the girl responded. "Although you might as well call me dirty cloud lately. All I do is clear these silly trenches day after day. I never get to do anything else." Flying Cloud grumbled bitterly as she cast a scathing look at the hoe lying on the ground. "So why are you here?" she asked excitedly. "It has been so long since I got to talk to any-one my age."

"A friend of mine is sick, and Tasker, the small man, thought your shaman Walks with Clouds might be able to help him," Jane explained as she sat down on the ground across from Flying Cloud.

"Oh," Flying Cloud said with a groan in her voice. "Grandpa has been very bitter since we came to live down here. I don't think he'll help anyone from the surface. He put the cursed dream catcher near the pit to stop anyone from finding us."

"But my friend will die," Jane exclaimed. She looked around nerv-ously, hoping her voice wouldn't carry too far. When no one seemed to notice, she looked back at Flying Cloud. "There must be some way to help him."

"I could probably do it," Flying Cloud said suddenly. "My grandpa's taught me almost everything he knows. Let me think." She paused a mo-ment as she tapped her chin with two fingers. "I'd need my medicine bag and my grandpa's bandolier bag. Both are in our wigwam. However, if I go back there now, my mom would wonder why I was returning so early, but I might be able to convince her that Grandpa was sending me on a trip to Salteaux." She stood excitedly. "Come on. I can get you into the village without anyone seeing you. Once I get my bags, we can free your friends and go."

"But . . ." Jane started as Flying Cloud twisted her braid excitedly.

"Oh, please, you must let me help," Flying Cloud pleaded. "If I stay down here any longer I'm going to go crazy. My people were not meant to live underground. Even though life is safe here, I want to see the sky. I've never even seen the sun. I was born down here. My mom told me about lakes and rivers and forests and so many things. I want to see them." Close to tears as she clung to Jane's arm and looked at her emploringly.

"Fine," Jane agreed. "But I have to know you can cure Jacob's poi-son."

"I can do it," Flying Cloud insisted, "of course I can," with such con-viction that Jane gave in and smiled.

"How do we get Tasker and Eriunia out?" Jane asked as the native girl led her to the edge of the strand of trees and along the wall of the cavern until they were out of sight in a low spot. They walked towards the village until the ground started to rise again, and then entered a larger gully dug into the ground by repeated movement of water.

"They'll leave them in the earth lodge until Grandpa gets done meeting with Red Bull, the shaman of the Salteaux. Today is their meeting day, and it normally takes them a while to settle any disputes that have come up between our bands," Flying Cloud explained as she popped her head over the top of the gully bank and looked around for anyone who might be watching. "Wait here. I'll bring you some clothes to wear." Without waiting for an answer, she scurried over the top of the gully and disappeared.

Jane waited nervously in the gully for what seemed like forever before Flying Cloud appeared again and slipped into the water channel.

"Here, put these on over your clothes," Flying Cloud said as she handed a buckskin dress to Jane, and then started to weave feathers and strips of hide into her hair. "Your hair is pretty, but it is too light. If anyone gets too close, they'll see you're not one of us. From a distance you may be fine."

They worked for a few more minutes on her disguise until Flying Cloud turned her around and examined her critically, "It should work." She motioned for Jane to scramble up the side of the gully. Together they approached the first of the wigwams. "The two you seek are in the earth lodge. I'll get the guard to leave the door. You sneak in and wake them up." She reached under her dress and pulled a small leather bag from around her neck. Reverently she handed it to Jane and motioned for her to slip it inside her dress. Then she pulled two small sprigs of a leafy plant from inside a pocket hidden inside her dress and handed them to Jane "That's my medicine bag. Put a leaf from each of these under their tongues. Then set the medicine bag over their hearts. This should wake them from the dark sleep. I need to get into Grandpa's wigwam and get his bandolier bag. He never carries it unless someone's sick." Flying Cloud pointed to the earth lodge. "Hide over there while I get Running Wolf to leave the door."

"How are you going to—" Jane started.

"Oh, that's easy," Flying Cloud said with a wide smile that showed her perfect teeth. "He'll do anything for me." She leaned over and whispered to

Jane in a conspiratorial manner. "He likes me." She winked as she hitched her buckskin up until it was well above her knees, and then walked around the corner of the earth lodge. When she was certain Running Wolf was staring at her with wide eyes, she suddenly fell to the ground and groaned. In a rush of footsteps, the young warrior was kneeling at her side. Flying Cloud peeked around the crouched warrior and saw Jane slip inside. Flying Cloud groaned one more time.

"Are you all right?" Running Wolf asked.

"I think so," Flying Cloud murmured as though waking for a daze. "Can you walk me over to Grandpa's wigwam?"

"I shouldn't leave my post," Running Wolf said worriedly. He looked around, no one was in sight. With the small tribe struggling for its existence, there were few enough hands as it was. Everyone was busy.

"You won't be gone long," Flying Cloud pouted. "And I feel so faint. Please help me." She swooned weakly in his arms.

"All right," Running Wolf said as he made up his mind. He glanced back one more time at the entrance to the earth lodge, and then helped Flying Cloud to her feet and slowly walked her across the village to her grandpa's wigwam.

* * * * *

"TASKER?" JANE HISSED as she slipped inside the earth lodge and looked around. She spotted the slumbering forms almost immediately. The Ojibwa warriors had put them on skins near the center of the earth lodge. They were still sleeping soundly. Jane hurried over to where they lay and pulled the medicine bag from under her shirt. Gently she laid it over Eriunia's heart first, put a leaf from each twig under her tongue and waited, hoping Flying Cloud was right that the medicine bag would break the dark sleep brought on by the dreamcatcher.

Just when she was about to give up and try the procedure on Tasker, Eriunia's eyes fluttered open. She looked around at her surroundings. The earth lodge was empty of any type of furniture, the only decoration to break the uniform brown of the interior being a small fire pit surrounded by bear and deer skin rugs.

"Where are we?" Eriunia asked quietly as she smiled at Jane and rose carefully to her feet.

"Hold on," Jane replied as she arranged the medicine bag over Tasker's heart and tucked two leaves under his tongue. Then she stood and faced the door because there was a tap of footsteps and then a shadow filled the door. Jane motioned for Eriunia to lay back down and then leapt into the shadow filling a corner and huddled into a small ball. Running Wolf's head popped into the opening a moment, and then disappeared again. Jane heard voices—Flying Cloud talking to the warrior. She hoped she could keep his attention.

"Uh," Tasker groaned slightly as he awoke and looked around. He saw Jane crouched in the corner and immediately followed her eyes to where she was staring towards the only exit of the lodge. He clamped his mouth shut and watched the hide that hung in the door for any signs of movement. When nothing happened, he rose to his feet and motioned her over.

"I found someone who can help us," Jane whispered. She stopped talking as the voices at the door grew louder. They listened intently as Flying Cloud's more shrill voice argued with a much deeper slower voice.

"We need to find another way out," Tasker muttered as he heard the voice of the old shaman rise to contend with his granddaughter. "It seems I misjudged Walks with Clouds. He's no longer interested in returning to the surface at all."

The three of them examined the back wall of the earth lodge. The timbers that held the outer walls in place were sturdy but the branches woven between the big supports were brittle and old. They gave way freely when Tasker pushed against them. He went about clearing a path for them to escape through the ever-widening hole in the back of the lodge.

"She'll meet us out near the mine pit," Jane whispered as she helped Tasker push away the last of the branches. The dwarf slipped through the opening and nodded to her as he reached back in and helped Eriunia out. Jane followed them both through the opening, and together they ran to where the irrigation gully started. Moments later they were running as fast as they could away from the village and towards the distant cavern wall.

CHAPTER SIX

Spirit Wolf

Y OU NEED TO HELP THEM, GRANDPA!" Flying Cloud said in frustration. She spoke loudly, hoping that Jane would hear her and find a way out of the earth lodge.

"No! They're from the world above," Walks with Clouds muttered. His face was set against all argument, and the fact that his granddaughter was blocking his path and begging with him made him all the angrier. "The world above is filled with traitors, liars, and thieves."

"I don't want to stay here. I want to see the world above and feel the wind on my face," Flying Cloud shouted back. "I've never even seen the very thing I'm named after." Tears were running freely down her face now as she broke into a very real argument she had used with her grandfather many times. She loved the old shaman, but he refused to attempt to return to the surface, and she could not stay underground any longer.

"Never!"

"What will you do with them?" Flying Cloud asked through her sobs.

"They'll be given to the river," Walks with Clouds replied without any emotion in his voice. "The river can judge them."

"You would kill people we don't even know?" Flying Cloud asked quietly.

"If it means keeping our people safe," Walks with Clouds said firmly. "Yes, I would." He turned to Running Wolf. "Guard the lodge until tonight. We'll send them down the river at crystal fade."

Flying Cloud looked at the great sun crystal and gauged the time, less than two hours for them to gain enough of a head start that her grandpa could not catch her. It wasn't much time. She hadn't expected him to return so quickly, but it seemed that Red Bull had fallen ill, and the meeting between the two shaman had been postponed for several crystal days.

When she was sure that her grandfather was not going to enter the earth lodge, she turned away from him and fled across the village with her

46

face hidden. She couldn't afford for anyone to see the triumph on her face. She had slipped her grandfather's bandolier bag from his wigwam while her grandmother slept and hidden it near the edge of the village. Now she dodged behind a dwelling and grabbed the leather bag from under a stack of old hides and slipped her head and arm through the wide leather strap. The beaded bag was heavy, but she still managed to run well enough with it around her neck. Soon she neared the edge of the cavern.

"Flying Cloud, over here!" Jane called from the edge of the tunnel. Jane looked out over the edge of the cavern. The village remained silent, but she was willing to bet that it wouldn't stay that way for long.

"I have it," Flying Cloud said breathlessly as she nodded to Eriunia and Tasker.

"Jane, I'm not so sure about this," Tasker muttered. "How do we know ' she can cure Jacob?"

"We don't have any other choice," Jane replied. "Flying Cloud says she's worked with her grandfather for years and knows much of what he does. Besides, you heard him, he won't help us. In fact, he was going to kill the two of you."

Tasker frowned, "I hope for Jacob's sake you're right." With no other options open to them, the four turned and hurried down the tunnel away from the Lost Ojibwa and towards the mine pit leading back towards the surface.

"They know," Flying Cloud said suddenly. She had taken her medicine bag back from Jane and tucked it inside her own dress as they approached the cursed dream catcher. "Wait for a moment while I counter the curse long enough for us to pass safely. She reached into her bandolier bag and pulled out a small wooden pipe. After taking a deep breath from the pipe she leaned as close to the dream catcher as she could and exhaled a great cloud of smoke that turned a silvery blue as it floated up through the air and gathered around the dream catcher. "Go!" she urged them.

Jane dashed under the dream catcher and felt a momentary urge to sleep. Then it was gone as the smoke took on a life of its own and formed a barrier around the dreamcatcher. She grabbed onto the handholds and began climbing as fast as she was able, wanting nothing more than to break out of the underground mine and see the sky once more.

They were nearing the top when a shout echoed up the pit from under them. Jane paused to look down.

"Don't stop," Tasker urged as he tapped her leg with his hand to draw her attention back to the climb. "Walks with Clouds is not happy."

Jane scrambled up the last twenty feet and rolled over the edge of the pit, she jumped to her feet and turned around to help the others into the chamber. There was a blast of hot air from the pit as Eriunia and Flying Cloud rolled over the top. Then they all looked back down. An eerie red glow filled the bottom of the shaft, and Tasker stumbled back with his face ashen in color.

"He has summoned a nightmare," Tasker muttered. "The old fool truly has lost his mind."

"What is it?" Jane asked curiously. The smell of brimstone coming from the pit was horrible, and she wrinkled her nose as she stepped back.

"An evil creature," Tasker explained. "The offspring of an evil creature that spent its days marking when people in these lands would die."

Flying Cloud gasped and covered her mouth with her hand. Her dark eyes were wide and filled with fear.

"Can you slow it down?" Tasker asked her. "We need to get out of here and into the sun light above. It'll be weakest there."

"I think so," Flying Cloud replied. She opened the bandolier bag and rummaged for a moment. Seconds later she pulled a thick ball of what looked like silvery threads from it and motioned for them to spread out around the pit. "Just wrap it around something and then throw it back."

Under her direction, they wove a silvery net over the top of the pit, and then tied the string off around a stone that stuck up from ground.

"What is it?" Jane asked as they stepped back.

"Webbing from a silver spider," Tasker replied. "Although I have never seen so much in one place, it must have taken months to collect."

"Will it stop whatever is coming?" Jane asked.

"Maybe," Tasker replied. "It was well worth trying."

"Let's go," Flying Cloud said as she closed her bag and turned away from the shimmering net. "I don't know how long this will last."

They ran along the mine tunnels with Tasker in the lead, fleeing as quickly as they could. Behind them the evil creature must have reached the magical webbing. Jane heard a scream of rage that nearly made her lose her footing. The cavern shook as the creature fought against the silver strands. The sounds added wings to their feet.

The passage angled upwards until finally they were standing in a strange chamber Jane couldn't remember passing through on the way down. "Where are we?" she asked as she gasped for breath.

"I told you the way out would be different," Tasker said. He looked around, seeking some sign of an exit but was unable to spot any way out of the chamber. "The Portsmouth Mine is just above us but how to find the exit is beyond me. Flying Cloud do you know how to leave the mine?"

"I've only heard rumors," she admitted. "I was never allowed to leave the village. My parents and grandparents said the surface was no longer for our people. They refused to let me even see the sky or the clouds that I was named after."

"But there must be a way to leave the cavern," Tasker insisted. The room around them was about twenty feet wide and almost circular, the walls painted with many symbols and pictures he assumed told a story.

"Let me read for a moment," Flying Cloud murmured as she walked to the edge of one of the picture graphs and ran her finger along the row of paintings. Her lips moved slowly at first and then more quickly as she passed around the room. "It is designed so that no one person can open it. It was built this way so that no one could run away and give away our last sanctuary to the enemy."

"What do we do?" Tasker asked.

There was a sudden explosion of noise from deep in the mine. Flying Cloud lurched, her face paling considerably. "It is coming," she said weakly. "Look here on the wall." She pointed to a small depiction of the Ojibwa eagle and pushed on a spot in the wall just underneath the painting. There was a clicking sound. She motioned for the rest of them to spread out. "Go find the same paintings on the other walls, we need to depress all switches at once."

Jane raced across the chamber and searched through the red pictographs until she found the one she wanted. Just below the eagle was a small indentation in the wall. She pushed in on the stone and was rewarded with a loud clicking sound. Around the area two more clicks sounded, and they were rewarded with a horrible shuddering and grinding sound from above their heads. Then light from the outside flooded down on them and a series of stone steps emerged from the floor and led up to a single spot on the stone wall above them. They all released the switches and raced to the steps.

"We don't have much time," Flying Cloud said. "According to what I read on the walls, the steps only stay in place for a short time before the switches need to be pressed again." Flying Cloud vaulted up the steps. At the top a blank stone wall confronted them. She halted before it.

"How do you open it?" Tasker asked as he felt the shift in whatever gears were controlling the steps.

"Jane, pull the eagle feather from your hair," Flying Cloud ordered. "Push the quill into that hole at the bottom."

Following her instructions, Jane ripped the eagle feather free, wincing as several of her blond hairs clung to the feather when she pulled it from her head. She searched around the bottom of the door for a moment before finding the tiny hole and pushed the feather into it. As the steps began to slowly retreat, the outer door they had seen under the eagle on their way in swung open. Flying Cloud leapt out into the bottom of the Portsmouth Mine.

"Come on!" she shouted back at them.

Eriunia followed her with a graceful leap that moved her out of the way. She turned and caught Tasker's hand as he leapt and almost fell short. His arms flailed wildly until she pulled him over the edge, and they both turned and stretched out the hands to Jane.

"Jump!" Tasker shouted. The steps had sunk almost half way back into the ground, and he leaned over the edge reaching back to her.

Jane took a step back, lined up her body, and hurdled forward using all of her strength to reach up and catch Tasker's outstretched hand. The sturdy dwarf caught her fingers and immediately reached out with his other hand and wrapped it around her wrist. They both began to slide back into the chamber until Eriunia and Flying Cloud grabbed his legs and pulled with all their might. Suddenly a second weight was added to Jane's body, and she looked down. The face that looked up at her nearly made her lose her grip. She screamed loudly. Running Wolf looked back up at her but his face was distorted and filled with rage. It was as though Walks with Clouds had taken a nightmare of a wolf and forced it into the body of the young warrior. His eyes flashed yellow and his mouth was bared in a snarling rage.

"Help me!" Jane screamed as she slipped back slowly into the cavern. Suddenly she was flying up and out of the hole, and all of them tumbled free of the door and collapsed to the ground, before them the stone door swung slowly shut and finally closed with a dull thud.

Tasker was the first to his feet as his body felt full of energy. With hope of getting Jane out fading he'd given in to his heritage and spoken a Dwarven rune of power. He could feel the earthen strength of his people fill him for a moment, giving him the strength to jerk the entire group out of the mine, but now the surge faded quickly. Once more he felt the façade that he had spent years building up slip ever so slightly. His beard, kept trimmed short, doubled in length, and wrinkles appeared around his eyes. Oddly, his time on Jane's side of the Divide had shown him that her side understood te basic principle that he had just used. Power could not really be created or destroyed, simply changed. It was a law of the universe.

"We made it!" Jane whooped with a smile and wrapped Flying Cloud in a great hug. Before she could continue a snarling came from near the stone steps leading out of the mine. She turned to see Running Wolf crouched near the stairs.

"My grandfather has lost control of it!" Flying Cloud shouted as she scrambled frantically to where the bandolier bag had fallen from her. Running Wolf's body was convulsing as the wolf nightmare took control of his mind and body. A looming dark aura around Running Wolf resembled a wolf and its eyes glowed yellow and red.

The warrior lunged toward Tasker, slapping the dwarf away as if sensing the dwarf was a greater threat to him than the others. As the dwarf rolled away, he turned towards Eriunia and leapt at her. But the elf was more agile. She turned her body to avoid the projected claws and slipped around the spirit creature, delivering a sharp blow to its side.

"I'm not completely defenseless in this world," Eriunia said with a grim smile. "This is what all elvish people are trained to do—battle evil spirits that try to enter our safe haven."

"Keep him away from me," Flying Cloud cried, continuing to rummage through the bandolier bag, frantically pulling items from its depths.

Jane grabbed up a rock from near her feet and heaved it at Running Wolf. She was rewarded with a snarl as the stone thudded against his shoulder. Then the nightmare charged her, and she suddenly wondered at the wisdom of her action.

"Careful girl," Tasker shouted. He leapt to his feet and launched himself at the warrior as it passed. The dwarf wrapped his arms around Running Wolf's legs and held on tightly. The warrior stumbled, fell and howled loudly. A flurry of blows rained down on Tasker's back and head, but he ignored the pain and held on while Jane scuttled back to where Flying Cloud was still arranging things on the ground around her.

Eriunia ran over to Running Wolf and used her palms to land heavy strikes on the physical body that the evil spirit was possessing. "Weaken the body and the spirit will follow," was the elven adage. She put all her skill to work. Two strikes on Running Wolf's neck caused his legs to go limp for a moment and gave Tasker a chance to regain his strength. Then her strong arm encircled the warrior's neck and squeezed tightly as his hands beat against her, trying to break the iron grip locked around his neck. The strength of the warrior was immense. Try as she might, Eriunia's grip began to falter.

"Help me," Running Wolf groaned suddenly in a weak voice. "I can't stop it. Please help me." He sounded so weak and scared that Eriunia nearly loosened her grip, but then the snarling struggle returned. With a sudden burst of strength he lunged to his feet pulling her off the ground with him.

"Hold him still!" Flying Cloud shouted. Suddenly, Flying Cloud leapt over to him and jammed a small object into his mouth. Running worlf made a low groan as the mixture of oils, minerals, and other mysterious components were absorbed into his blood. Then he went limp. "He's still awake but he cannot move for now."

"Release me."

Jane gasped as the unearthly voice hissed out from Running Wolf's mouth.

"You have to banish it back to the underworld!" Tasker insisted.

"I know!" Flying Cloud exclamed. She grabbed a small bowl and added three compounds into it and mixed them together. Once the mixture began to react she sprinkled it over Running Wolf's entire body. The effect was immediate, and the spirit bound into Running Wolf howled in rage and then fell silent.

"You can't stay here!" Flying Cloud said aloud to the nightmare spirit. She watched as it stopped trying to escape the bound set upon it by Walks with Clouds.

The creature looked at her and nodded, then spoke. "We will meet again someday, you and I. Next time, you may not be so fortunate."

"Go back to the abyss that you came from," Tasker growled. He struggled to his knees and crawled to where Flying Cloud was looking down at her friend.

"It may kill him," Flying Cloud said through her tears.

"That thing is evil, pure evil," Tasker replied. His strength was returning and he reached over and helped hold Running Wolf's arms down. Already the substance that Flying Cloud had used to immobilize the warrior was beginning to wear off.

"I'll do it," Flying Cloud replied. She pulled another small item from her bag and forced Running Wolf to open his mouth. Carefully she dropped the powder into his mouth and looked at Tasker. "This is going to stop his heart from beating for a few moments. Once that is done the nightmare's connection to this world will be broken and it will be forced to return to the abyss."

Jane gasped, "What of Running Wolf?"

"If we're lucky, I can bring him back," Flying Cloud replied. She placed her hands gently on Running Wolf's forehead and watched through the tears as he stopped struggling and his breathing slowed. After about a minute he lay quiet and seemingly at peace with the world. The moment he stopped breathing the nightmare screamed loudly and vanished in a puff of smoke.

"There! It's gone," Jane cried out. Even though they had been fighting the warrior she prayed desperately that he would survive. "Bring him back."

Flying Cloud leaned over and opened Running Wolf's mouth. Carefully, she removed the small stone and through it into a corner. She dug in her bandoleer bag and pulled a small vial of liquid. She forced several drops into his mouth and the leaned over and started what looked to Jane like modern CPR.

"Here, I can help," Jane exclaimed. She leaned over his chest and began compressions.

"We need to push the drops into his blood," Flying Cloud said.

They worked for almost five minutes straight before Running Wolf suddenly gasped loudly.

"Stop," Running Wolf gasped. He struggled to sit up and looked around. "Is it gone?" He shuddered violently as he thought about the creature that had taken hold of him.

"Yes," Flying Cloud replied tiredly.

"Thank you," Running Wolf said weakly.

"We cannot stay here," Jane said. She hated pointing out the fact but Jacob's life was hanging in the balance and she desperately wanted to return.

"Go. I will be fine," Running Wolf said. He waved them off. "I can feel my strength returning. Besides, I'm not returning to the village. Now that I 'm free, I am going to see the world outside the village."

Flying Cloud sagged to her knees as a great wave of weariness rolled over her. Fighting through the exhaustion, she carefully returned everything to her bag. Suddenly she wondered about the wisdom of volunteering to help, what if her strength and knowledge were not enough?

Jane hurried to where Tasker was struggling back to his feet. He dismissed her helping hand.

"I'm all right, girl," Tasker muttered. "We need to get back to the mushroom circle before the Naga has us for lunch and return to Stockton Island." The trip back up the hundreds of steps leading out of the Portsmouth Mine was much longer than Jane remembered the journey going down. When they finally arrived back at the surface, she sat down on the ground and wearily shook her head. Her legs shook with exertion, and beads of sweat dripped from her face.

Flying Cloud looked up at the sky in amazement. Suddenly a wave of fear passed over her. It was so open. The blue sky was empty of clouds, and the sun blazed brilliantly, bringing a wave of warmth over her that she found disconcerting.

The sun was high in the sky but beginning its downward track. Jane struggled back to her feet the moment her breath returned and her heart stopped racing. To the south where Serpent Lake lay an inarticulate roar came, and she shivered as the sound bore into her.

"How do we get past it?" Jane asked. She followed Tasker into the woods. Flying Cloud and Eriunia walked side by side behind them listening carefully to the dwarf as he spoke.

"I had hoped it would've returned to the water by now. The legends of the Nagas tell of them being fond of sacrifices. This creature will allow us passage if we can offer it something it wants," Tasker said as he walked. As he talked the distant shores of Serpent Lake were visible through breaks in the trees.

"What do they demand?" Jane asked curiously.

"Normally human blood, but that is out of the question," Tasker said with a dry smile. "He might be satisfied with a gem of great worth." He rolled the stone he had taken from the bottom of the mine in his hand and hoped it would be enough.

They struggled up a small rise just south of them, and Jane found her strength waning again and gasped when they reached the top. The Naga had not only emerged from the lake to watch over the mushroom circle upon their return but his thirty-foot-long body was now coiled around the perimeter of the mushroom circle. As they stood watching its great hooded body, it turned to them and spoke.

CHAPTER SEVEN

Ambushed

I SEE YOU THERE," the Naga hissed slowly. Despite its human looking face the eyes were those of a serpent and they flickered across the hillside watching them. "Why have you disturbed my home?"

"It was not our intention to disturb you," Tasker replied. "We however needed to meet with the Lost Ojibwa and this was the closest method of travel. Will you allow us to leave in peace?"

"No!" the Naga hissed as its coils undulated around the circle and broke off several of the smaller trees. "You must pay a price."

"What do you demand?" Jane asked suddenly. The sun was moving in the sky much too rapidly for comfort, and they had to move fast if they were going to save Jacob.

"Something of value to you . . ." suddenly the Naga stopped speaking as its eyes were drawn to a nearby stand of trees.

Jane and the others looked around, wondering what the creature would take that they could offer. She reached into her pockets, searching, but only the heart stone from the mine entrance was still there.

"There's no way it would want that," Jane muttered to herself. Still, she decided to try, and she pulled the stone out and held it up.

"What is that?" Flying Cloud asked.

"One of the stones from below in the mine," Jane replied.

She held it up for the naga to see. "What of this?" To her amazement the creature seemed fascinated in the colorful stone and slowly its great head lowered down.

"That is a special stone," the naga said softly. "Not for its rarity, but that stone guards a great secret for the people who once called these woods home."

"Will you take it and let us leave?" Jane asked. "My friend is dying and we have to hurry."

"Very well," the naga replied. It reached out carefully with the tip of its tail and wrapped it around the stone.

With one last look at them, the great snake turned and slithered back towards the lake.

"Take my hand quickly," Tasker shouted as he reached out to each side. There was a rattle of stones and the snapping of small trees as the Naga slithered away.

Jane grabbed Eriunia's hand and Tasker's with her other hand. She held on tightly waiting for the dwarf to open the mushroom circle and take them away from the approaching creature. She looked over to where Flying Cloud should have been standing and realized that the girl was still a few feet away bent over something on the ground.

The tunnel flashed around them. Tasker guided them back to Stockton Island. Jane began to see the myriad paths that existed below the surface of the earth. Thousands of passages and pathways led to every corner of the world and to every land where mushroom circles exsisted, pulling power from the magnetic lines that surrounded the earth. It was a built-in transportation network. One simply needed to know how to operate it.

A few minutes later they emerged from the ring on Stockton Island, and Jane breathed a sigh of relief, it was late afternoon, but they were still in time. As the others emerged from the tunnel, she hurried them to their feet and towards the fort. Tasker ran as fast as his short legs could carry him followed by the three women. All were gasping for breath when they finally broke from the forest and came within sight of the fort. There was a scurry of activity as the gate swung open, and Tasker collapsed on the ground just inside the structure. "Go!" he shouted to them.

Jane led Flying Cloud across the compound. They threw open the door of the smaller building and rushed inside. Bella was floating over the thrashing form of Jacob, who still lay on the table, his face pale and his breathing labored. The fairy net she had woven around his body to hold him still had frayed in places, and the strain of holding it left the fairy pale. She fluttered weakly above his head.

"Quick," Bella said. "I can't hold him much longer, but if I release him the poison will run its course."

Flying Cloud rushed to Jacob's side and looked at the handsome boy with a worried expression. The poison was nearing his heart. She needed to move quickly. If it reached his heart, she could do little to save him. Her hands trembled as she removed the medicine bag from around her neck and held it over Jacob's body. She prayed aloud a moment, asking the great spirit who fashioned the world for help. Finished, she placed the medicine bag on Jacob's chest over his heart. Immediately the healing powers of the medicine bag began to flow into him. The poison stopped moving towards his heart and began slowly retreating. The battle was fierce though as the poison gave ground grudgingly. Soon sweat soaked Flying Clouds brow and she felt a great weariness coming over her.

When Flying Cloud thought the poison was pushed back to the initial wound, she dipped her hand into her Grandfather's bandolier bag for what she had gathered from Serpent Lake—a small vial filled with Naga blood she had taken from a depression in a rock. Ever so carefully, she motioned for Jane to remove the bandage from Jacob's wound. There was an sharp intake of breaths at the sight of the wound. His side was literally turning into stone. She allowed a single drop of the Naga's blood to fall into the wound, hoping what she had sensed earlier would be true.

The effect was immediate. Jacob's breathing slowed and his limbs stopped thrashing about. Between the Naga's blood and the power of the medicine bag, the poison was driven from his body until it actually fell to the floor and soaked into the dirt.

"It's done," Flying Cloud said in utter exhaustion, collapsing.

Jane leapt forward and caught the native girl as she fell. With Eriunia's help she arranged Flying Cloud carefully on the nearby cot and returned to Jacob's side. He was breathing peacefully now and the wound on his side where the bullet had struck him was completely healed except for a small scar. The fairy net that Bella had spent the day holding in place dissolved slowly. Then the exhausted fairy fluttered over to the weapons rack on the wall and sat down on a cross beam.

"Thank goodness that's over," Bella murmured.

Jacob woke with a start and looked around, "What happened?"

"You came through the Divide with a poisoned bullet wound," Jane explained. She smiled at him as he sat up and looked around. "We spent most of the day trying to track down someone to cure you." She pointed over to where Flying Cloud was resting peacefully in the cot.

Jacob shook his head once to clear it. "It feels like I've been fighting against a cloud that filled my mind with cotton," he said. The girl lying on the cot was nearly the same age as Jane and nearly as pretty, with jet black hair and tanned skin. Her clothes looked to be straight out of every picture he had ever seen of native American attire. Jacob swung slowly to his feet and walked to where she was sleeping.

"Thank you," he whispered quietly not wanting to wake her up. He was rewarded with a sleepy smile and a flutter of her long black lashes as she looked up at him for a moment, then slipped back into sleep.

"We need to pack our things and move," Tasker interrupted suddenly. The dwarf rushed through the door with a wild look in his eyes. "This is better than we could have hoped for."

"What is?" Jane asked. She was tired and just wanted to sleep even if it was only for a few minutes.

"Commander Darkback has landed his troops on the southern half of Stockton Island," Tasker explained. "Thankfully Puck took the initiative and prepared our forces to flee. Which we're going to do but not in the direction everyone thinks we will'."

"What?" Jane and Jacob asked in unison.

"Just get everything we can carry and head for the ships," Tasker bellowed loudly.

"What's going on," Flying Cloud asked sleepily as she turned to look at the dwarf. Her eyes caught on Jacob and her heart fluttered. He was handsome. She felt immediately drawn towards him.

"If his troops are here, that means he doesn't know we have ships, and he left their fortress unguarded," Tasker replied. "This is our chance to appropriate his ships and take Madeline Island, while stranding him here." Tasker chuckled while he scooped up the few things he had managed to salvage from the fort and turned towards the door. "Well, come on!"

Jacob gave a start, "Can I help you?" He reached to Flying Cloud and offered her his hand. He felt his face blushing as she smiled at him and reached out daintily with her own hand to accept his assistance.

"Time to go," Jane muttered under her breath as she watched Flying Cloud stand slowly and wobble back and forth while Jacob tried to support her. "Sheesh." She turned away and reached out her hand to Bella, who fluttered slowly into her palm and then accepted a spot on her shoulder.

They followed Tasker out the door and through the side gate. Along the path a steady stream of Puck's goblins and freed slaves headed to the dock. When they arrived at the docks, the area was a hive of activity. All the ships had returned and were slipping into what space was available along the piers. Everyone was carrying supplies down the wooden planks and into the bellies of the waiting ships.

"Come on," Tasker pointed to one of the larger ships. This one sported a pair of masts and a dozen oars on each side. A large contingent of fighters were already aboard, and more were loading. When they also went aboard, Tasker said, "We have a special duty tonight." He smiled as they walked across the deck and entered the single door which led into an open cabin that seemed to also double as a chart room.

Jane looked around as the ship rocked gently around her. The movement of the waves made it difficult to focus, but she hoped she would get used to it quickly. They went to a long table bolted to the floor. Tasker crossed to a closed cabinet and pulled a long sea chart from the container.

"Don't worry. This map doesn't cross over to anything," Tasker said as he saw Jane's eyes widen. "We're going to take two ships and swing south along the shore. Puck and a few of the best goblins are still ashore and are going to lead Commander Darkback on a merry chase before using the mushroom circle to escape. Once we get close to our goal, I have a special mission for each of you. If everything goes according to plan we'll sail away with four Ironships."

"I can't go with you," Jacob said suddenly, and immediately all eyes were drawn to him with a clamor of questioning voices.

"What do you mean, Jacob?" Jane said as she walked to where he was standing with his arms folded.

"They have my mom," Jacob said quietly. "If they were willing to try to kill me, they'll kill her. I have to make sure my mom's safe." He hung his head, "I know you all went through a horrible time to save my life, but I have to make sure my mom's safe before I do anything else. Think about it, Jane. What if they targeted your grandparents?"

Jane stumbled to a halt and stared at him. Her eyes got wide suddenly, and she turned to Tasker. "I have to make sure my grandparents *are* safe," she said, her voice filled with panic. "I've been gone all day. What if they tried to take my grandparents while I was gone."

"Go. Make sure they're safe," Tasker said. "We'll see to the castle here. Be careful. The Adherents are taking this further than they ever have before. Trying to kill people across the Divide is a sign of how confident they're becoming."

"We'll be back as soon as we know everyone's safe," Jacob promised as he nodded to Jane. "Your house or mine?"

"Mine," Jane replied. "Your house is most likely still being watched. We can sneak into Grandpa's house from the back. No one will see us."

* * * * *

SHE STEPPED THROUGH the Divide. A moment later the trees and privacy fence of her grandparent's backyard came into view. Jacob appeared beside her a second later, and they both looked around, but the yard was dead quiet. The small gazebo her grandpa had built two years ago was sitting empty, and the night sky was filled with lights.

"What do you think?" Jacob whispered. There was only one small light on inside the house and no sign of movement. The night was silent.

"Let's go see if Grandpa Able's there," Jane replied. "Considering how we vanished from the police station, he's probably pretty worried."

They crept up to the back of the house. Jane slid the patio door open. All was silent. The house seemed empty. Then she heard a muffled sound from the bedroom on the main floor. Jane dropped all pretense of stealth and bolted for the bedroom door. She flipped lights on as she ran and threw the door open, calling for her grandmother and grandfather. Her heart pounded, praying that they were safe.

"Jany?"

She breathed a sigh of relief as Grandma Kay looked towards her and shaded her eyes against the sudden burst of light. "Where have you been, girl?" she asked. She was sitting up in bed with her reading glasses perched precariously on the end of her nose. The iPad Jane and Jacob had spent time setting up was in her lap, and she looked down at it and smiled to whoever was on the screen.

"Yes, she just ran into the house," Grandma Kay said. "I don't know where she was. I can ask her." She looked up at Jane, "Your mom wants to know where you were all day?"

"She wouldn't believe me even if I told her," Jane muttered. She crossed to the bed and sat down on the end of it with a grimace. Fully knowing what was about to happen, she picked up the iPad and turned it around so the built in camera was facing her. There on the screen, was her mom's worried face staring back at her.

"Where were you?" her mother said. "Your grandfather called here this afternoon and said you disappeared from a police station with some boy."

Jane shook her head, "It's all right, Mom. It was a misunderstanding. They let us go when they found out the drugs weren't his . . ." Jane stopped as another wave of shock passed over her mother's face followed by an eruption of tears.

"DRUGS!"

"Mom, we had nothing to do with it!" Jane nearly shouted back. "I promise you, we had nothing to do with any of it. Someone's trying to set Jacob up." Jane stopped, it was obvious her mother was beyond reasoning. Her face disappeared from the camera, and Jane heard sobbing and the sound of her mother blowing her nose loudly.

"Where's Grandpa?" Jane asked her grandmother finally. "He can help explain this."

"He's out looking for you two," Grandma Kay explained. "He came home with some wild story about how you disappeared from the police station and told me to stay in the house while he went looking."

"I'll call him," Jane muttered. "Jacob, can you grab my phone?"

Jacob heard the request and trotted over to where the stairs led up to Jane's room. His sense of apprehension grew as he mounted the stairs, and his mind told him something was wrong. *This is too easy. The Adherents know where they live. Why have they left Jane's grandmother here by herself?* He slid the door open. Suddenly a dark shape slammed into him and knocked him back towards the stairs. In an effort to stop his backward momentum, Jacob grabbed the railing and managed to pull himself back up the stairs before he fell, even though a piece of banister came away in his hands.

"You," the Adherent muttered. "I killed you once already."

"I don't die that easy," Jacob muttered as he faced the Adherent. The man was drawing a weapon from behind his belt. Jacob launched himself forward, swinging the hunk of banister hard. It struck the gun as it was rising and knocked it from the Adherent's hand. Jacob then crouched and used his shoulder and upward momentum to strike the man again. That sent him flying backwards into Jane's room and into the darkness.

CHAPTER EIGHT

The Frying Pan

JANE HEARD THE CRASH from the upstairs and hurried towards the door. She heard Jacob yelling something. There was a land line phone on the wall in the kitchen. Jane lunged across the open space and grabbed at it. She punched in 911, and only then realized there was no dial tone.

At the top of the steps Jacob was grappling with a robed figure. Suddenly he broke free and leaped to his feet. As the Adherent—and Jane knew that's what it was—rose, Jacob swung wildly with a section of banister and struck the man hard across the back. The blow sent him tumbling down the stairs until he finally came to a halt at Jane's feet.

"You're mine," the Adherent started to say, but his eyes went wide.

When the Adherent fell down the stairs, Jane had grabbed a cast iron frying pan off the stove. Just as he shouted at her, the pan connected with the side of his head, and his eyes rolled back.

"That's the second time you got to knock one of them out," Jacob complained as he hurried down the steps and grabbed the Adherent by the front of his robe. "We need something to tie him up. He might know if they took my mom."

Jane ran to the garage and grabbed a roll of duct tape from her grandpa's work bench, and then hurried back into the house. She handed the roll of tape to Jacob, and then rushed to her grandmother, who was standing weakly in the door looking terrified.

"How did that man get into the house?" Grandma Kay demanded.

"I don't know, Grandma, but I'm going to call the police and Grandpa," Jane replied. She helped her grandmother back to her bed and then ran upstairs to retrieve her phone from where she had hidden them. Her first phone call was to her grandpa. He sounded hugely relieved when he answered.

"Are you two all right?" Grandpa Able asked. "Stan about lost it when we returned and found you missing and his officers stunned. There

64

was blood on the floor, and he had everyone he could contact looking for the two men. It turned out that the DEA hadn't send anyone over and the local office claimed they knew nothing about any of it."

"Just come home, Grandpa," Jane begged when she could finally get a word in to the conversation.

"I'll be there in ten minutes," Grandpa Able replied.

When Jane returned to the main floor of the house, she found that Jacob had leaned the thin Adherent up against the thick support post at the bottom of the steps and taped him to it. The half used roll of tape was on the floor. They waited for Grandpa Able to return and the other man to awaken.

"You hit him pretty hard," Jacob chuckled. He had taped the Adherent's hands together and then taped his arms to his sides. Then he'd wrapped about twenty layers of tape around the man's entire body and around the sturdy support pole. Even when the Adherent woke, he'd be immobile.

"Grandpa will be here soon," Jane said. She walked back into the kitchen to set the frying pan in the sink. She turned around and glanced out the living room window, and her blood ran cold. A police cruiser parked in the shadows down the street under a tree. The inside was dark.

When she pointed it out to Jacob, he said, "I wonder who it is?"

"Might be one of those officers Stan was suspicious of," Jane said.

"Or one of the guys setting me up," Jacob growled. A few minutes later, Grandpa Able's car rounded the corner and pulled up to the garage. A groan from behind them signaled the Adherent beginning the return to consciousness. With unfriendly eyes outside, Jacob pulled the cord on the blinds as they turned away from the window.

"What's this?" Grandpa Able exclaimed when he entered the side door and saw the ruins of the banister on the floor. His eyes widened as he saw the man taped to the pole, "Stan will be very happy to lay his hands on you," he said to the bound man.

"Grandpa, there's a police car down the street," Jane said. "Any idea who sent it?"

"Stan said he was sending a couple of officers to watch the house. He was livid when we returned to the interview room," Grandpa said.

"I think you should call him and let him deal with this guy," Jane said.

The Adherent was now fully awake and struggling against his bonds but the tape would not give. Thankfully Jacob had checked the man's coat before restraining him and the small round anchor pinned to his jacket was now tucked safely into his own pocket. "Might want to tell him to bring a restraint jacket though. I think he's insane."

"Is Grandma all right?" Grandpa Able asked quietly as he looked towards the bedroom door.

"She's concerned, but okay," Jane replied.

"What's going on here, girl?" Grandpa Able asked quietly.

"We need to find Jacob's mom," Jane replied. "Grandpa, this has to do with Jackie."

His eyes went even wider for a moment but then a look of steel entered them. Grandpa Able walked over to where the Adherent was struggling and grabbed the corner of the tape covering his mouth. His hand was strong and firm as he tore it loose and then grabbed the man by the throat and held him still.

"Where's my granddaughter?" Grandpa Able said in a quiet voice. His hand formed a vice around the Adherent's throat, and the man's face began to turn purple as he struggled for air. Slowly he released his grip and waited as the man regained his breath. "Now understand me, I want to know about my granddaughter."

"Cain has her, old man," the Adherent snarled as he tried to pull his head away.

"She's alive?" Grandpa Able muttered in disbelief. "Who's Cain?"

"You will never know," the Adherent spat back.

"Where's she, Jane?" Grandpa Able said over his shoulder. "I have a feeling you know more than you've said. Your grandma and I thought something odd was going on around here. Do you know where she is?"

"I don't think you'll believe me, Grandpa," Jane said slowly. "But I think there's a chance of getting her back. First we need to make sure you, Grandma, and Jacob's mom are safe."

Grandpa Able turned towards Jacob, but before he could say anything, the Adherent laughed maniacally.

"You're too late to save her, boy," the Adherent burst out. "We sent her across the Divide, and you know what that means. She's stuck there."

Jacob shouted something unintelligible and lunged towards the man, but Jane and Grandpa Able caught him and held him back. When he was able to control his emotions again, Jacob grabbed the tape and stopped the flow of taunts coming from the Adherent.

"We know where she is, Jacob," Jane said to him, and she glared at the robed man. "We can get her back."

"Is this place . . . this Divide . . . close," Grandpa Able asked as he picked up his cell phone and dialed Stan's number.

"Sort of," Jane admitted.

"Do you think you can help Jackie and Mrs. Tanner?" Grandpa Able said.

"I think so," Jane admitted hesitantly not sure what her grandpa was going to do. She watched him as he turned and opened a cabinet in the kitchen and retrieved a locked gun case. Slowly he loaded the army issued .45mm and chambered a round, "This gun and I have seen many things in the jungles I was never able to explain. I do know that each time I was in danger, this gun and I managed to come through. You two go find my Jackie, and Jacob's mom. I'll keep this one here and make sure no one comes near Kay or me." He dragged a kitchen chair around so it was against the wall but still allowed him an open view of the living room door and the front door.

"What about mom?" Jane asked.

"I'll see that Stan sends someone to watch over her," Grandpa Able promised.

Nearly three hours had passed now since they had returned, and Jane wondered if Tasker and his group had achieved their goal. "Grandpa, Jacob and I are going to disappear in a few minutes. We need two or three days to try to save Jackie and Jacob's mom. Can you keep people from starting a search for us for that long?"

He nodded. "Go save her."

Jane pulled her map from inside her jacket and unrolled it, "Jacob, I moved my anchor to here. I need you to get me an anchor back to Madeline Island."

"All right," Jacob answered. He glared at the Adherent one last time then stepped into the Divide. The last thing he heard was a muffle gasp as Grandpa Able watched him vanish.

"It's all right, Grandpa. He's fine," Jane said as she turned back to her grandpa.

"I saw that happen one other time," Grandpa Able said suddenly. "I was scouting someplace where Americans were not supposed to be, in Laos near the border of North Vietnam. Deep in the jungle I happened to come across an ancient ruined city that the locals called the Cradle of the Vanishing Ones. They refuse to enter the place after dark and most times wouldn't even go near it during the day. I scoffed at them and started into the ruins looking for signs of Viet Cong scouts. There was a massive temple shrouded in the jungles overgrown with vines, I thought it was a hill the first time I saw it."

Jane looked down at her map and noticed that Jacob had figured out how to place an anchor. It was there at Madeline Island waiting for her. Still she waited while her grandpa continued.

"I went into the ruins thinking it would be a good place to camp for the night. I woke up in the middle of the night when the moon was at its highest point and the light shone through the ceiling onto the floor of the temple. There was a set of stairs there that hadn't been there before. I went down to investigate, and at the bottom of the stairs I found a room filled with treasures—strange and ancient things beyond your wildest dreams scattered across the floor. I took one thing out of the room to prove I'd been there. It was a small carving of a dragon made out of gold with two tiny emeralds for eyes. As I was leaving to mark the spot on my map, I heard someone coming, so I hid. A short man with a beard appeared carrying a whole armload of treasure. He added it to the piles. Then he walked over to a stand and set down a golden book on a stone pedestal. Then he vanished just like Jacob did. Just vanished into thin air. Soon after I returned, we pulled out of Vietnam, and I never had the chance to to go back. As far as I know the treasure is still there."

"I wonder if Tasker knows anything about this," Jane muttered. "I'll be back soon, Grandpa, hopefully with Jackie." She hugged him once and then stepped back and entered the Divide to where Jacob was waiting. They would jump to Madeline Island and then use smaller jumps to find the fleet.

Grandpa Able looked around the room and shook his head as silence descended, except for the continued struggles of the Adherent. "Tasker. That's what the little man in the jungle had said before he vanished," Grandpa Able muttered. "I remember now. He said, 'I can't let Tasker or Cain find this.' That's exactly what he said to himself."

He reached for his phone but then changed his mind. *Might as well give them a head start before I start this*, he thought. He double checked Jacob's taping job and then went into the bedroom and to take a nap so he would be well rested when he finally called Stan and turned the taped man over to him.

CHAPTER NINE

Taking an Ironship

TASKER GATHERED THEM AROUND and began speaking quickly, pointing to various spots on the map and making each of them repeat what he had told them to do until it was ingrained. "We don't have any more time. This is our one chance."

Jane and the others nodded.

"It's time!" Echoed a shout from outside the door.

"All right, it's time to begin," Tasker said. He nodded to Jane, "Remember, an easy touch with your pen and then, if you continue moving the lines lightly, the fog will last longer."

"I can do it," Jane muttered. She knew her job, but it wasn't what the others would be doing. For a moment, she glared as Jacob, Eriunia, and Flying Cloud left the cabin. Bella glanced over at her before flitting out the door as well. Jane sat down and bent over her map. Slowly the Divide came into view, and she swooped in close until she spotted the swirls along the shore where the ships were located. Ironships were especially resistant to any sort of tampering, but that did not keep her from carefully drawing her pen across the area. Slowly, outside, a thick bank of fog developed and swept in around the small fleet.

Tasker looked down at her map approvingly.

"It's ready," Jane announced a moment later. "I'll keep it in place as long as I can." She nodded to Tasker, "I have this. Go!"

Tasker ducked out the door and ran to where the keen-eyed goblins were squinting into the rolling waves of fog billowing across the lake and the nearby island. "Keep us on course. I don't want the defenders on the Ironships hearing us until we draw alongside their hulls. Jacob, if you would, please."

Jacob gave him a thumbs up signal. Then he disappeared into the Divide. It took him only a moment to enter the blackness and find the map he wanted. Jane's familiar map stood out among the others. Hers was the only one he could safely use, and he had no wish to be trapped

70

somewhere outside or inside the Divide, so he examined hers until he found what he was looking for. Seconds later the cold iron deck of the nearest ship appeared around him and a surprised sentry stared at him. The man's mouth opened for a moment, but Jacob hit him with his best shoulder tackle. The man gave a startled yelp as he tumbled over the railing and hit the water below with a splash.

Jacob crouched next to the railing and looked around. Another shadow moved in his direction, and he vanished into the Divide. A moment later, he appeared behind the second Adherent. Without any warning or outcry, the second man vanished over the side into the lake water below. Satisfied that he had disrupted the watches enough on this particular Ironship, Jacob vanished into the Divide and located the second in the line of warships. This time he examined the ship for a moment before locating the first of the Adherents keeping watch. The ship was similar to the *William Irvin* moored in Duluth but had a smaller scale than the 1930s ore carrier.

The front of the ship was raised slightly, and a thick, cold iron cannon had been mounted to the prow. Along the sides of the ship, the railings were shielded so those onboard would be protected during an attack. Two more cannons were mounted on either side, and they were similar in construction to the muskets seized from the Adherent guards. Jacob had seen pictures of muskets and had even seen a Civil War re-enactment once. He could not understand how the oddly shaped cannons managed to fire anything without exploding. Suddenly he heard an exclamation of surprise from behind him, and he whirled to see a shocked face staring out at him from within a black hood. The watcher was his age but thinner, and he fumbled with his musket as Jacob pulled his shield up in front of his body and charged.

With a muffled *thump*, Jacob felt a heavy blow strike his shield. He stumbled in his headlong charge, nearly falling to the wood deck planks. Strangely, the ship around him remained silent. When he was able to untangle his feet and look up, he saw the Adherent sprawled out on the deck in front of him. Jacob realized the shield had reflected the ball of energy and flattened the Adherent with his own round.

Jacob laughed under his breath as he dragged the unconscious figure into a dark corner. On a whim, he pulled the Adherent's black cloak off him and slipped into it. After retrieving the musket, he pulled back the hammer and re-armed the mechanism the way Tasker had shown him, and then started along the deck watching for his next target.

"Heral, is that you?"

Jacob paused as the wavering voice called out to him from the opposite side of the deck.

"This fog isn't natural, I tell you," the voice continued. "Something's going on. I just wish the commander would spring his trap already and be done with this rebel scum."

Jacob froze. *Is it true?* Was Tasker walking into a trap on the ships? He had to find out quickly, so he looked about the ship frantically seeking a way into the dark depths below. An open hatch nearby—Jacob scurried to it as the other watcher's footsteps faded along the ship's deck. He squinted into the darkness but could see nothing, so he started down the steps until a voice stopped him.

"Heral, get back up on deck. If the commander saw you trying to sneak down there, he'd have you strung up for good!"

Jacob hurried back up the ladder and stopped on the deck. This hatch on the ship was made of wood, but it was bound with cold iron, and Jacob grabbed the thick hatch and swung it shut. There was a sudden shout of surprise from below, and he fumbled with his musket before sliding the latch shut and locking it tight. Then he vanished into the darkness towards the first ship and the waiting ambush that would spell doom for Tasker and his raiders.

* * * * *

ANOTHER WEEK PASSED BY and Jackie smiled happily when she heard the key turn in the lock and she turned to see Carvin slip inside the cell and quickly close the door. He turned to look at her and there was a horrible purple-and-black bruise showing around his left eye.

"What happened?" Jackie gasped. She rushed over to him and dipped the edge of a piece of cloth in what remained of her drinking water. Carefully, she dabbed the cool cloth against his face and wiped the bits of blood away.

"My dad found out that I came to visit you the other day," Carvin said sheepishly. "I managed to dodge all but one punch. This was the one that got me."

"What a horrible thing," Jackie said. Her heart went out to him, despite the fact that he was still one of the people holding her captive.

She finished dabbing his face and suddenly realized how close she was to him. The kiss happened before she realized what she was doing and when she finally stumbled back from him they both looked away in embarrassment.

"I am sorry," Carvin stammered. "I shouldn't have done that."

"No I shouldn't have," Jackie started.

"I am going to find a way to help you," Carvin declared suddenly. He straightened his tunic and a determined look entered his face. "I swear it I will find a way to help you get back to your family."

With that he vanished out the door and fled, as the soldiers in the hallway locked the door.

Jackie sat on her bunk for a time, hugging her legs and trying to sort through the range of emotions that filled her. She remembered reading in her phycology class at the university about Stockholm syndrome and she wondered if that was the only reason she was becoming attached to Carvin. He seemed so different when compared the rest of the people she had met in this world.

CHAPTER TEN

Below Decks

I T'S A TRAP!" Jacob nearly shouted as he materialized on the deck of the wooden masked cargo vessel. In front of him, Tasker and his raiders were getting ready to board the silent warship before them. He had stopped for a moment in route and slammed the same hatch shut on the first ship and threw the locking bolt shut, drawing shouts of alarm from below.

"What are you talking about, boy?" Tasker hissed from where he was crouched on the deck near the railing. In his hands he held a rope with an iron hook and was ready to throw it across the short distance and tie off to the warship.

"Soldiers are on the decks below waiting to attack once we're on board," Jacob gasped. "I locked the hatches, but I don't know how long that will hold."

"You did well, boy," Tasker said with a smile. "Now that we know, we can finish what we came here to do." Tasker let his hook fly and caught with a solid thump on the side of the Ironship. All along the railing a dozen more ropes flew across the shrinking gap and all across the wooden ship strong hands heaved with all their strength to bring the ships together. There was a sickening crunch when the vessel met the Ironship. Immediately scores of rebels swarmed up the sides and spread out across the deck racing for the few other hatches that remained unlocked. Soon they were all secured, and a string of muffled shouts and calls came from below the deck.

"Puck, I believe it's time for your newest friend to make an appearance," Tasker said with a smile as they listened to the repeated shouts and blows coming from inside the ship's hold as the soldiers tried to escape.

Puck walked to the side of the Ironship and raised his right hand to his lips. A piecing whistle broke out a moment later and echoed across the water. Jacob looked worriedly at the hatch door, which was beginning to give way with the efforts of those below decks. Suddenly a beautiful sound broke over the side of the vessel and an odd looking creature landed on the side of the vessel. Jacob stared with wide eyes as the creature walked slowly towards the hatch way with her great deep black eyes fixed on the crumbling latch.

"Close your eyes, boy," Tasker said as he slapped Jacob on the side of the head. "And cover your ears, unless you want to live out the rest of your life in the depths of the siren's grotto."

Jacob followed his instructions, closed his eyes and turned his head away. He slapped his hands over his ears to lessen the effects of the song that was already working its insidious magic on the Adherents trapped in the ship's hold. Jacob risked one short glance as the latch gave way but instead of being attacked by dozens of soldiers he saw the first glassy eyed Adherent step from the ships hold and walk calmly to the edge of the ship and dive into the water below. He clenched his eyes tightly shut once more as the siren turned towards him and smiled. He nearly followed her, but Tasker's hand grabbed him, and he covered his ears once more.

When silence finally reined on the Ironship, Jacob stumbled to his feet and looked around shaking his head to clear the last echoes of the song. He could not tell what the strange looking woman had been singing, but he knew he'd nearly followed the Adherents over the side of the ship.

"When the Greeks finally got sick of losing ships, they drove the sirens out of their waters, and the remaining ones scattered across the world," Puck said sadly. "When I bargained for her help, I nearly stayed in her grotto myself." Puck looked over at Jacob and shrugged. "Once you enter a siren's grotto, you never leave it. Most never want to. They will die of starvation with happy smiles on their faces."

Jacob shuddered. All around him rebels broke into frantic activity as the looming shape of the second Ironship emerged from the fog just to the west. "I think the soldiers on the other ship are free," Jacob said to Tasker.

"Aye, lad, that they are."

"Will she . . . will the siren come back for them too?" Jacob asked hesitantly. "Because I don't know if I can handle that again."

"Lad, that siren will not be seen in this world for hundreds of years," Tasker replied. "She's taken her fill of this world for a long time. Temptation is a horrible thing. You almost gave in to her too. It's a good thing I was here to bring you back to your senses."

The second Ironship was less than five hundred yards away as Tasker brought the first ship around. A rhythmic sound came from deep inside the ship as he pushed a long lever next to the wheel forward and spun the wheel as tightly as he could. There was a shout of surprise from the other ship, and then the flashes of musket fire as the battle was joined against the rebel ship that had tied off on the other side. "Make ready to board the other ship!" Tasker shouted as he brought the Ironship around and aimed it straight at its sister.

Jacob read the name of the ship as he watched the gap close between the vessels, *The Black Stone*.

"Hail . . ."

Jacob nearly laughed when the sentries' eyes went wide with surprise to see a sister ship behave so. The three ships came together with a resounded crunch. Instead of a hundred Adherents claiming a swift victory, a swarm of goblins and freed slaves launched themselves into the back of the line of soldiers, firing their muskets at the wooden vessel floating forlornly fifty yards from the Ironship. There was a chorus of shouts and cries as half the soldiers were knocked unconscious or tossed overboard in the first few moments of the fight.

An hour later, the battle was over, and the few remaining Adherents were locked safely in the ships smallest hold, stripped of their weapons and robes.

"South to Madeline Island," Tasker called across the space that separated the two ships. Nearly six-hundred of his fighters were now milling about the decks of the two ships, many of them bent over their magical muskets while others showed them how to arm the devices and how to fire them. Two thick columns of black smoke soared into the air as the massive engines in the bellies of the vessels roared to life, and the water surged passed the great hulls.

"What of the other ships?" Jacob asked. "I thought there were two more out there somewhere?"

"We can't help that now," Tasker said. "If we sail now, we can be tied off to the harbor at Madeline Island before they realize who is on board."

"Shall I move forward and see what's happening at the castle?" Jacob asked. Jane was on the first vessel. He had seen her when she stepped out of the cabin and looked across the water towards him. He waved at her and smiled, but all she did was frown at him, and his wave faltered until he dropped his hand to his side. "I wonder why she's so mad?" Jacob muttered under his breath.

"I sent Flying Cloud and Bella to scout the island," Tasker said as he leaned closer to Jacob.

Suddenly the cannon mounted to the rear of the vessel boomed loudly, and they both turned to watch. Jacob stared with his mouth open as the massive ball of iron tore across the water and slammed into the prow of the next Ironship as it emerged from the heavy fog bank. The shot slammed into the hull near the water line. A moment later a second explosion tore through the side of the vessel, and it listed to that side almost immediately.

"Lucky shot," Tasker muttered as he watched the tiny forms of the Adherent soldiers struggle to keep the vessel from rolling completely over. "Go meet Flying Cloud and Bella and tell them we'll be there in less than two hours."

"How will I find them?"

"I think they'll find you before you find them," Tasker said with a smile.

Behind them the fourth vessel finally emerged from the last remnants of Jane's thick bank of fog, and in the distance their cannon roared to life. Jacob gulped as he saw the massive iron ball soar into the air but he quickly realized that the shot had no chance of reaching them. A cheer rose and a roar of taunts followed as Puck's goblins pointed and laughed. A few of the freed slaves even fired their muskets back at the last Ironship, but the shots traveled only a short distance before falling into the water.

Jacob stepped into the Divide and found Jane's map once again, he examined it for a moment until he spotted the outlines of the castle and then stepped out onto a hill on Madeline Island overlooking the castle. It was the one place he thought was tall enough to look down at the castle, and the top of the hill was covered with massive trees.

"Bella?" Jacob called softly, not wanting to announce his presence to anyone in the area. He looked down at the castle and watched for any sign of movement amongst the buildings that he had scouted when he returned from Bayfield a day earlier. No one moved inside the castle walls and only here and there an Adherent walked the ramparts. On the nearest wall a black-robed Adherent leaned over the wall looking down, when suddenly he cried out and clutched at his chest. With slow and exaggerated movements he toppled forward and fell over the outside of the wall and landed with a muffled *thump* on the ground.

"Well, I found Bella and Flying Cloud," Jacob muttered. He jogged down the hill and ran towards the wall, which seemed to grow bigger as he approached. It was built of massive reddish-gray granite stones. He figured the outer wall reached a height of forty feet. Two towers anchored the northern side of the outer wall, and they rose another twenty feet past the top of the wall. He saw Flying Cloud dragging the watchman from where he had fallen into the thick brush that still grew about fifty feet from the wall. Flying Cloud glanced at him but must have known he was coming because she continued dragging the figure of the Adherent into the brush and hid it under the thicket.

"Is he . . . ?" Jacob asked warily. He had never seen anyone who looked as limp as the Adherent was and he shuddered.

"Jacob, he would've killed us given the chance," Bella piped out as she fluttered through the trees and came to a halt on his shoulder. "We can't take chances if we're going to free all who are slaves of the Adherents."

He looked over into her serious eyes and frowned. "But isn't there some way we can handle this without killing people?" His eyes kept straying to the thick underbrush where Flying Cloud had finished hiding the body, and he shuddered uncontrollably.

"Jacob, most of these men and women joined the Adherents because they wanted to," Bella replied patiently. "Most have committed terrible acts against the people who refuse to follow them. Before you arrived here, when the Adherents were gaining power, they forced those they deemed undesirable to wear a white circle on the outside of their clothes. Those with the circle were targeted for many horrible things. Their money and homes were taken, they were driven from the cities and forced to live in separate compounds. Many disappeared into the northern mines. This all happened under the sight of men like this, men who, if they had stood up together, might have stopped all this before it started. Instead we sat back and said it wasn't our problem. We didn't want to get involved. Suddenly, when we awoke, the bully on the corner was not just a bully anymore but a tyrant."

Jacob's mouth snapped shut. He closed his eyes as the visions of the news shows he had seen last year in school talking about the Holocaust floated through his mind. His history teacher was Jewish and had gotten permission to show the older students old news reels of what had happened under the Nazi regime to his people. It was something that would stick with Jacob for the rest of his life.

"All right," Jacob nodded. "What does Tasker want us to do?"

"Clear the look-outs as best we can," Bella replied. She pulled the string of her small bow. "If anyone's captive inside, we could free them as the ships landed and create a little chaos."

"I'll take care of the captives," Jacob volunteered. "You clear the sentries."

Flying Cloud smiled to him as she walked back to where he and Bella were talking. "It's good to see you, Jacob," she said. "When I first saw you, I worried I might not have the strength to drive the poison from your body."

"I never got the chance to thank you," Jacob replied as he looked down into the great pools of her eyes. "Thank you . . ." he stammered as she stepped even closer. His face blushed furiously.

"You're welcome," Flying Cloud responded. She leaned up and kissed him lightly on the cheek, then stepped back and shook her head as if realizing that Bella was still present. "Stay safe."

"I will," Jacob replied. His hands were shaking as he raised his shield and stepped into the Divide. A second later he was standing outside the building he had seen earlier where the slaves might be held. The last bit of light was fading as he rounded the front of the building and hurried to the door. It was open. He took a deep breath, then slipped inside, into a small room with a tiny desk pushed against the wall.

Sitting at the desk with his back to the door was a robed Adherent, who raised his hand into the air, a motion for silence. "Wait. Do not interrupt me," he commanded imperiously.

Jacob shrugged. He pulled his sword and set it carefully alongside the man's neck with the blade where his eyes were drawn to it. Bella may be ready to end lives, but he'd avoid it if possible. Better to use the threat of violence than actually hurt anyone unless he was left no choice.

"How dare . . ." The Adherent's voice faded as the sword slid forward easily parting the material of his robe.

"Where are the keys to the cells?" Jacob asked quietly. He looked at the man and smiled. "My friends and I know most of your soldiers are away trying to trap us. Obviously that effort fell short. Now, I'm going to ask one more time for the keys to the prisoners' cells, and I want you to think really hard about the sword sitting on your collar. I should tell you also that those coming after me have no problem returning what you've done to them over the past years. You should be happy I'm here first."

The Adherent glared at him but very carefully removed a large iron ring from a belt secreted under his robes and turned very slowly towards the door that Jacob motioned towards. "Let's start with that one."

"You'll never get away with this," the Adherent muttered.

"Well, until someone proves to me that I can't get away with . . . this," Jacob replied, "let's just pretend I don't care." The door opened up into a long hallway with a dozen cells on each side. Each was locked and bound in cold iron. In the first cell were half a dozen cages, each containing a fairy. Many were sleeping, but they came to life quickly as the Adherent entered the room. Smiles filled many of their faces when Jacob entered after the man and motioned for him to begin freeing the fairies.

"Who else is held here?" Jacob asked as the first of the freed fairies weakly fluttered over to him.

"These cells were for those too strong or in our case too small to be held in the bigger areas. A couple of minotaur from the Greek islands are in the next cell over, and down at the end is an elf hunter, I believe," the fairy replied faintly. "I'm not sure about the other cells."

"Let's go get the elf first," Jacob said to the Adherent as he prodded the man in the back with his sword. Sullenly the Adherent led him to the end cell and worked the key in the lock, finally letting the door swing open. Inside was an athletic looking being that resembled a human except for his slightly pointed eyes and ears. He was sitting quietly on the bunk with his eyes closed as though resting. The moment the door opened he looked up.

"What's this?" the elf said with a smile as he rose gracefully to his feet. "The great keeper of the prison has finally met his match?"

Jacob stared openly as the elf suddenly grabbed the Adherent and artfully threw him against the far wall in a display of skill that would have left Steven Segal gaping. A groan and a crunching sound came from the Adherent as he slammed against the wall and slumped to the floor unconscious.

"My thanks, lad. I've been waiting to do that," the elf said with a smile. He held up the keys he'd deftly removed from the Adherents grip when he struck and pointed to the door. "Shall we go free the others and see if we can find a way off this accursed island."

"We don't need to find a way off right now," Jacob said with a smile as he looked at the unconcious Adherent on the floor. He stepped back and let the elf close the door. When the lock was secured, he started to turn away, but the elf caught his arm and held it in an iron grip.

"My name's Baenn. I have to find the princess," Baenn said as he held tightly to Jacob's arm.

"If you are talking about Eriunia," Jacob replied, "she's safe. We freed her from the cell where they were holding her. She's with Tasker and the others. She should be here soon."

Baenn smiled and released his grip on Jacob's arm. He danced a little jig in the middle of the hallway and motioned the human on. "Come then. Let us release the others and make ready for their coming."

He jogged to the next door and flipped through the keys until he found the one he needed. Moments later the chains which held two big horned human-looking creatures were freed. They offered their thanks in deep guttural voices. Jacob turned his head and looked up just in order to look the minotaur fully in the face, and the sheer amount of muscle on them was mind boggling.

When all of the cells were empty, Jacob looked around and noticed there was one more door still locked. He motioned to it, "Who's in that one?"

"I never saw them enter it," one of the fairies piped up.

"Open it up. Let's see what's inside," Jacob motioned for Baenn to open the door. He hefted his shield and readied his sword, unsure of what to expect. When the door swung open, a chill filled the air, and a pair of red-rimmed eyes looked back at them. The inside of the prison cell was completely made of cold iron, and when Jacob stepped inside he shivered.

"And who might you be? Do you come to fight me with your dragons scale shield and mighty sword?"

"I don't come to fight anyone," Jacob declared as he looked at the old woman with glowing eyes who sat calmly before him. He looked down at her curiously, and then opened his mouth again.

"Who am I, you ask?" the hag said before Jacob could say anything. She smiled at him. "I am the witch of Endor. I am she who has seen a thousand years. I am known by many names."

"We should leave her here," Baenn muttered. "She is evil."

"Good . . . Evil," the old hag said with a cackle. "Would you leave an old woman here in this cold iron cell to rot for the rest of her life?"

"What is she?" Jacob asked. He turned his head slightly to look at Baenn

"Banshee . . ." Baenn started. "Look Out!"

Jacob was about to answer when suddenly the old woman erupted from where she was sitting and literally flew from the room with a wailing shriek that drove them all to their knees. The sound bore into Jacob's ears so powerfully that he nearly blacked out. Then as quickly as it came, it faded, leaving them dazed. A shout of alarm from outside brought Jacob struggling to his feet. He glanced out the main door that led into the guard house and saw the remaining Adherents running towards there position.

"We have company coming," Jacob cried as he shouldered the front door and slammed it shut. A barrage of thumping sounds—the Adherents firing a volley of magical blasts aimed at where he had been a moment before. "Hold them off as best you can!" Jacob called to Baenn. "I'm going to go get help."

Baenn nodded as he grabbed a musket from the rack on the wall and tossed it to one of the men who had been freed. Jacob disappeared into the Divide only to appear a moment later outside the building and near the small iron guard house. He stuck his head around the corner and chuckled to himself when he saw how many Adherents were facing the guard house. Six, and those men seemed confused by the odd absence of the other soldiers to help them. On the far side of the castle he saw Bella and Flying Cloud making their way slowly towards the nearest of the distracted soldiers, so he turned back to the building before him. The door was solid iron and set on posts with a mantel designed to withstand anything.

"She said it would cut through anything," Jacob muttered under his breath as he drew back and swung his sword with all his might at the massive lock holding the door shut. He braced his body against the coming blow and was pleasantly surprised when the blade passed through the iron and severed the lock completely. There was a dull thud as the bottom of the lock fell to the ground, and Jacob reached out and pulled with all his might, drawing the door open slowly. Inside the small iron building he found a perfectly round dragon's egg that glowed with an inner fire. Carefully Jacob approached the egg and hefted it in his arms. It was surprisingly light and about twice the size of a basketball. He hurried from the iron building and took a deep breath. He was tired from running in and out of the Divide. He needed someone to guide him through the mushroom rings.

"Bella," Jacob said out loud. He needed the fairy now, and she was on the opposite side of the castle. He was growing very tired and needed his last bit of energy to make it through the gauntlet of musket fire.

CHAPTER ELEVEN

Into the Mushroom Circle

E TOOK OFF RUNNING as he clutched the great egg. As he passed a long building against the wall opposite him, suddenly the door opened, and four more Adherents boiled out of the portal. His legs burned with effort but he forced away the pain and kept moving. Confusion helped him get to cover, but a volley of shots splattered against the iron building, one so close he nearly dropped the egg. After a few deep breaths, Jacob sprinted away towards where he had seen Bella last. A shout came behind him, and he ducked his head and ran for all he was worth. Amazingly he made it to the side of the bigger building where Baenn and the others were making their stand and slipped around the side.

"Bella!" Jacob risked being heard and was rewarded with a shout of warning from a sentry still pacing the walls. The Adherent raised his musket but suddenly clutched his shoulder and dropped his weapon. With a frightened look on his face he ducked inside the tower next to him and disappeared from sight.

"Jacob!" Flying Cloud shouted back as she waved from where she and Bella were hidden behind a stack of firewood piled near the wall.

Jacob looked around before he ran toward the stack of firewood. It looked clear so he sprinted as only a star football player could. He heard a shot and felt the energy ball as it closed in on him. Then he was flying head over heels in the air towards the firewood. His side felt like it was on fire, and the egg flew from his grip. Time seemed to slow as he caught a glimpse of the egg falling towards the rocky ground. It disappeared, and he crashed head first into the chunks of timber.

Flying Cloud saw the musket blast as it exited the weapon and flashed across the castle grounds. She saw it strike Jacob on the side and send him flying, and even worse, she watched the crimson dragon's egg jarred from his grasp. She lunged forward with her arms outstretched and got her hands and arms under the orb. It bounced once on her arms and tapped against the ground slightly, then rolled to a halt almost against her face. From inside the egg she felt a slight shudder as the life within the hard shell rebelled against the treatment it just endured.

There was a chorus of shouts across the gravel, and then Flying Cloud scrambled back behind the stacked logs while Bella launched an arrow from her bow.

"Get Jacob," Bella shouted.

"I'm trying!" Flying Cloud called back as she set the egg carefully on the ground. She glanced around the wood and noticed that Jacob was crawling weakly towards their shelter, his arm and leg on the right side flopped weakly as he pulled his body with his left arm. She crawled around the side and grabbed Jacob's outstretched hand and pulled him back until they were both protected by the firewood once more.

"Thanks," Jacob said as he lay on the ground with his head resting in her lap. "I didn't think anything could feel this bad." His right side felt like it had been hit with a sledge hammer. His muscles ached and head hurt.

Flying Cloud touched his face gently and wiped away the dirt smudges from his face. She reached out to him and placed her medicine bag on his chest once again. Slowly the reddish bruises and burns across the right half of his body faded, and Jacob began to move his arm and leg again.

"Are the Adherents coming this way?" Jacob asked when he could finally move. He raised his head and stood carefully. "Thanks, Flying Cloud. I feel much better." He reached down and helped her to her feet, noticing how soft her skin felt in his hands.

"No, the prisoners you freed have been firing muskets from the doors and windows," Bella replied. "We're pretty much at a stalemate. They have the entrance to the jail well controlled, but we can harass them enough that they can't move very well either."

"Bella, can you take us through the mushroom ring to Ringrose Peak?" Jacob asked as he picked up the egg. "If we can return this to Yerdarva, she'll be able to help us."

"I think I can," Bella replied. "The trails under the world are twisted, and traveling through them takes a quick eye and an even quicker mind."

"There's a small gate leading outside," Flying Cloud pointed to the north of where they were. "We should make for it now before more Adherents arrive and block our escape."

"Are you ready?" Jacob asked.

"I should be asking you if you're ready," Flying Cloud said with a smile.

"Whatever you did to me I feel like a million bucks," Jacob said as he stretched. They heard a shout from across the grounds, and two energy shots slammed against the wall behind them.

"Watch out," Bella said with a snort. She leveled her bow but held her shot as the only target she could see was well beyond the range of her weapon. Her quiver was more than half empty already, and they still had hours left before midnight, so she saved the arrows she had remaining.

"Ready?" Jacob asked them. He had managed to pull his shield and sword over to where he could grab them. He checked the straps one last time. "Stay close and stay behind me. The shield will block the shots." He placed his sword back in its sheath and once again took up the egg.

Flying Cloud and Bella crouched behind Jacob, awaiting his signal.

"Here we go!" Jacob called. He bent almost double and began to move quickly towards the distant gate. It was less than one hundred feet, but it was the longest race he'd ever run. Balls of energy careened off his shield and splattered into the wall behind them while other shots dug furrows into the ground and spat dirt into the air.

Jacob saw one Adherent stand to take a better shot, but he was knocked back by a musket volley from the well-defended block house.

"We made it!" Flying Cloud laughed as they skipped out the small gate and ducked around the edge of the wall away from the view of the castle grounds. The castle was on the southern arm of the land surrounding Big Bay. As they ran down the sloping hill, they entered an area filled with swamps and pools of standing water.

"Ick!" Flying Cloud muttered as they forced their way through the swamp, quickly getting covered in mud and muck. When they finally broke free, Bella was the only one not filthy. The only thing clean on Jacob was the egg, which he had held high in the air.

"Come on," Bella cried. "It's not too much further."

The mushroom circle was on the northern half of the island. They ran through the dark forest and stamped through heavy brush until it finally came into view.

The circle was atop the only hill in the area, and it stood about two hundred feet above the lake surface, Jacob panted wildly as they ran up the slope. By the time they reached the top, he was completely winded, and his side hurt worse than running sprints during football practice.

"It's over here," Bella said excitedly. She pointed across the top of the hill to where a small circle of trees watched over the mushrooms.

"Wait a second," Jacob replied as he turned and looked back at the castle. Two big Ironships were pulling into the docks, and they could see the small figures of Tasker's freedom fighters leaping down to the docks and rushing into the castle. But far out on the lake he saw an ominous grouping of lights that looked similar to those on the Ironship Tasker controlled.

"I think someone is coming," Jacob muttered. "And I don't think it's good."

He turned and rushed to the mushroom circle, "It's all up to you Bella." He grabbed Flying Cloud's hand and put his finger out to where Bella could grasp the digit in her tiny hand. With a flash of light, the mushroom circle opened and the landscape around them was gone.

* * * * *

THIS TIME JACOB'S TRIP through the tunnels that connected the mushroom rings was much different from when Tasker had taken them through it. They careened off walls, and twice Bella was forced to do what Jacob thought looked like a huge loop to catch a turn they had missed. When the growing circle of light finally showed that they were approaching an exit, Jacob breathed a sigh of relief. Then they were forcefully expelled from the mushroom ring, and Jacob sprawled out on the ground holding the egg high to avoid damaging their precious cargo.

"We made it!" Bella squeaked, and she sounded surprised.

"I knew we would," Jacob said with a big grin as he climbed to his feet. "I always had faith in you."

Bella blushed and fluttered over to sit on Flying Cloud's shoulder. Her face reddened, her wings curled around her and hid all but the tips of her toes behind them.

"Come on, let's deliver Yerdarva's egg," Jacob said excitedly. He reached out to Flying Cloud and took her hand. Together they jogged around the lake towards the distant gash in the great mountain. The energy that Jacob had gained began to wane as they ran, and he struggled to even keep pace with Bella's excited fluttering.

"Young Runner!"

Jacob stumbled as a great voice shook the mountain and brought them to a halt. He stood with his legs trembling as the great red dragon emerged from her lair and moved towards them in great leaps. When she arrived, he carefully held out the egg to her and watched as she daintily took her offspring in her talons and turned back towards her lair.

"Wait here," Yerdarva instructed them. Somewhat slower then she had arrived she walked back to her lair and disappeared inside.

They waited for nearly an hour until the dragon emerged again with a leather pack held in her mouth, she walked to where they were and laid the pack on the ground. "Here is food and water. You need to rest while I arrange the protection of my offspring. Then I will show you the foolishness of kidnapping a dragon's child."

"Cain's forces are closing on Madeline Island. They'll soon have Tasker trapped behind the castle wall there," Jacob explained as the dragon turned back to her mountain again.

"We will make it there in time, Runner," Yerdarva said quietly. "That I promise. Once my baby is safe, we will rain fury on Cain's forces." Her voice went from quiet to thunderous and drove the three of them to their knees.

"Let's eat and give her the time she needs," Flying Cloud said as she put her hands on Jacob's arm. "You need some sleep too. It'll help you get your strength back."

"All right," Jacob muttered. He enjoyed being near the Lost Ojibwa girl but each time she touched his arm or smiled at him, he still saw Jane's face frowning at him. He was torn. Both were beautiful and sweet and he liked each of them for different reasons. Jane was exciting, and she was from his world. Flying Cloud was quiet and mysterious, but she was from this world. It made him feel like she was forbidden, but that only made him more interested in her.

They ate fresh fruits and nuts and drank fresh mountain spring water out of skins. Yerdarva had provided several blankets, and when they had finished eating and had brushed off much of the dried muck, they all lay down and were asleep in no time.

* * * * *

TASKER, ERIUNIA, AND JANE ran up the docks, across the wooden structures and through the gates into the castle, following the disorganized horde of goblins and freed slaves. The few Adherents still moving about were captured immediately, and a shout of surprise came from the beleaguered defenders inside the block house.

"Braun," Eriunia called out when the elf man stepped out of the block house. He waved to her and smiled widely. "It's good to see you. Does this mean my father has re-opened the passages to this world?" She offered her hand as he knelt and kissed the tips of her fingers reverently.

"No," Braun replied as he rose to his feet and motioned to the rest of his fellow defenders out of the block house. "A group of trackers begged to be sent out to find the lost princesses, but the Adherents knew we were coming. Thirty set out from Tir Na Nog. The five of us were taken captive, and the rest were scattered to the winds."

"Something feels wrong," Jane muttered suddenly from where she stood behind Tasker. She turned and walked away from the small cluster of freedom fighters and the happy reunion. The air felt chill to her, and the night seemed gloomy without Jake or even Flying Cloud. He could be so irritating and yet so likable at the same time. Her mind wandered as she slowly climbed the narrow steps just inside the gatehouse that led to the short squat tower on the left. The stones were thick and looked old despite the claim that the castle had only recently been built. She leaned on the outer parapets and looked out over the moon-lit lake. Away from the lights and smog of the city, she was able to see for miles. Below her vantage point and set in the walls were eight ports where cannons could be fired, four of them sported the flared barrels similar to the muskets, and she shuddered to think of the effect that a blast of that power would do if fired against their rising rebellion.

"Nothing here," Jane muttered. She was about to turn away from the quiet lake when a flash of light drew her eye. It came again out across the waves, a small flicker of light. Then it began to spread as a long line of warships marched out of the depths of Lake Superior from the east.

"TASKER!" Jane shouted. "Get up here!" Jane turned back to the water and counted until she reached twelve, a dozen of the great iron behemoths. The advancing force was more than a match for their two Ironships even if supported by the big cannons built into the fortress.

"What is it?" Tasker asked as he hurried to the top of the wall. His voice fell as he looked out at the advancing forces. "Close the gates and get our two ships around the far side of the island."

"We're horribly outnumbered and have a six to one ship disadvantage." Puck pointed out. "We can't win this fight."

"FINE! Go if you want, but I stop running here!" Tasker erupted. He stamped his foot on the unyielding stones. He turned to the rebels gathering below and motioned for silence. More than five hundred faces looked up at him from inside the fortress, five hundred men, elves, and dwarves along with a sprinkling of other races all waiting for him to speak. "This is where we make our stand. It appears, however, that we have stung Cain more than we thought. He has decided to bring part of his Lake Huron Fleet north to deal with us, but this time he underestimates what we have accomplished. He thinks he can simply walk over the Prison Isles and turn us all back into just that—prisoners." Silence filled the courtyard as the gathered rebels waited for him to continue. "Do you want to go back to being forced to work for the black robes?" There was a muttering of anger that slid across the gathered rebels.

"But we cannot win against that fleet!" Came a shout from the back of the gathering.

"So we go back to running?" Tasker replied. "NEVER! We moved each time the Adherents came close to us and look what it's gained us. Our families are taken prisoner and used against us, our children grow up never knowing the fathers who died in the iron pits, our wives and mothers outlive us and our own children weep over our graves."

Now the courtyard was silent but the upturned faces were filled with determination.

"We have the strong walls of a fortress between us and them. We have eight guns that have longer range, and we have the desperate courage of those who have been pushed to the breaking point," Tasker said quietly. Despite his low tone, his voice still carried to every part of the gathering. "Every one of you is worth twenty Adherents. I say we hold this fortress and break his fleet here and now. They may not even know we are here yet. That will be their downfall."

The tremendous shout that followed literally shook the stones under Jane's feet. She felt a surge of excitement and courage that took her by surprise. She looked back and watched as the two ships they had captured slipped away from the port, leaving the docks empty. Out across the water, the advancing force halted for the night. Below them in the courtyard there was a burst of activity as Braun took command of the forces and began directing teams of rebels into the gun emplacements.

"Have you ever been in a battle?" Eriunia asked as she stepped to Jane's side and put a hand on her shoulder.

"Well, no," Jane admitted.

"It's very dangerous yet exciting," the elf princess explained. "Stick near me. I'll do what I can to keep you safe. After all, you are our secret weapon."

"What?" Jane asked but she stopped as she looked down at the inner pocket that held her map and pen. "Oh, I suppose so, but Tasker said that magic of the maps wouldn't work against cold iron."

"Oh, it may not work against the iron but there are plenty of other things that you can throw at those ships," Eriunia replied. "For example, as long as they remain in the open water you can make it very difficult to aim their cannons at our walls."

Suddenly a world of possibilities opened up before her. Jane smiled.

"They may steam right into the harbor," Tasker said as he turned back from the frenzy of activity below them. "We have all the lights doused around the fortress. That'll make it hard for them to see who's manning the walls."

"What then?" Jane asked.

"Braun's going to retrain the cannons so they're all pointed directly at the moorings," Tasker said with a smile. "If we can get eight of their ships into port, we can go a long way towards balancing this fight."

The tension on the walls was thick as the rebels took up positions atop the wall and around the eight cannons and waited while the advancing Adherents slid closer and closer. Jane took to walking the walls nervously as the night slipped away and morning began to lighten the sky. Out across Lake Superior, the Adherent fleet slowed as it approached the fortress and seemed to be waiting for first light to enter the harbor.

"They know something's wrong," Jane muttered darkly to herself. She nervously gripped her pen and looked down at the map spread out before her inside the protection of a small room above the gate. She glanced out a window that was no more than a narrow slit and watched as the ships continued to drift closer.

"No, they don't," Tasker replied. "Too little time has passed. This was probably a naval exercise planned out before we had the unfortunate timing to interrupt. We can use this to our advantage. Imagine if half of his Lake Huron Fleet goes missing. It'd be a great blow to Cain's power across the entire great lakes area."

"Here they come," Eriunia burst out from where she was watching just outside the shelter. Her eyes were narrowed and she motioned with her hand towards the ominous fleet sitting less than a mile from the docks. "Looks like half of them are moving in and the rest are sitting."

"Blast," Tasker muttered. "Well, it can't be helped. If we can get half of them into port we'll take that. Are the boarding teams ready?"

Eriunia's eyes swept along the hidden alcoves along the docks. She spotted the dark forms clinging to the back of barrels and crouched under the wooden docks. "Looks to be."

"Send a runner to Braun. Remind him only to target the center piers," Tasker told her. "I want the two outermost ships captured with the least amount of damage."

"He knows," Eriunia replied. "He's fought more battles than all of your soldiers combined."

Tasker huffed but didn't press the point. Instead he looked out over the top of the narrow slit and watched as half the fleet slipped towards the waiting piers. At even points along the docks, he had stationed rebels dressed as Adherents and bearing muskets. He needed the advancing forces to feel safe and at ease as they came towards the waiting trap.

"They're tying off the first Ironship," Eriunia said quietly to Jane. "Get ready with your map to move against the others."

"Remember, Jane," Tasker hissed without taking his eyes from the vessels below them, "they're built out of cold iron, and it's all but impervious to our skills. Don't try anything with the ships themselves. Send the wind or better, the water."

"I understand," Jane answered as she stared at her map and readied herself.

"Now they are all tied off," Tasker signaled to Eriunia. The elf nodded and repeated the signal to those crouched behind the thick stones.

BOOM.

Jane jumped as one of the big guns below them in the wall thundered out its welcome to the unsuspecting Adherents. Then the world around her faded as she entered her map and examined the tiny images of ships gathered off shore. There was a swirl of activity on the map around the fortress, but she forced her mind to ignore it and begin sketching in the oncoming storm. She started with a line of waves that began north of the fleet and sent them south. She was hopeful as she watched the waves start rolling towards the ships. When they struck the iron hulls, Jane realized fully the power of cold iron in this world. The drawn waves struck the hulls, but many of them died immediately.

BOOM!

A second round of cannon fire shook the walls. Now an answering barrage as the Adherents tried to swing their own cannons up to cover the walls. Seeing her first attempt dissipating, Jane brought her pen across the map again and a wall of fog slowly rose blocking the ships from view. Then she tried for wind and sketched a massive funnel cloud across her map and aimed it at the ships.

"That's the idea girl!" Tasker shouted above the dim of the cannons, which were now firing as quickly as the crews could reload.

The massive water spout struck the clustered ships with the force of a hurricane, and Jane watched as the massive vessels bounced off each other and slammed about mercilessly across the heavy surf. However, the leaching power of the cold iron still worked against her, and slowly the water spout died. Six Ironships began to belch black smoke and scatter in six directions.

Two of them steamed into her wall of fog and vanished from under the cover of her own summoned blanket. Jane struggled against the pull of her map for a moment and realized that the efforts were taking a toll on her body. She needed to do something quickly. This time she drew in a thing she had seen before, the image of a cloud with a great face in it and strong winds blowing out of it from the south to the north.

"Careful, girl!" Tasker shouted but it was too late. She had released her creation across the water, and it had taken a life of its own.

Jane stumbled back from her map covered in sweat and looked about, suddenly aware that smoke and noise filled the fortress. She managed to pull herself to the window and looked down at the docks. The four Ironships that had moored in the middle of the pier were half submerged, and the few Adherents still moving were throwing off their robes and leaping into the water and attempting to swim away. The outer two ships seemed to have fared better, and the southern one looked to be completely in rebel hands. The one furthest north was still held by the Adherents, and she could see the battles raging across its decks as Puck's goblins and Tasker's rebels fought to take the ship from the determined defenders.

With a shout, Tasker and Braun led another contingent of rebels across the docks to the contested ship. They scaled the thick ropes holding the ship in place, and the elf swept across the deck taking anyone who rose to challenge him.

"Jane!" Eriunia shouted from the door. "We need to get everyone under cover quickly."

"What happened?" Jane replied as she stumbled to the door. Her flagging strength returned slowly, and she was just able to walk.

"Your storm's going to stick around for a while," Eriunia replied with a grim smile. She pointed out across the lake where the other two Ironships were just emerging from the cover of the fog and beating their way south toward land. Filling the sky behind them was a massive bank of clouds that blocked all view. They were an angry dark-green and great bolts of lightning flashed connecting earth and sky. In the middle of the clouds was the image of a face, and out of its mouth came great gusts of wind.

Chapter Twelve

The Wrecked Ship

B Y ODIN'S BEARD, GIRL," Tasker muttered when he finally returned from helping secure the last of the ships. He was soaked to the skin as were most of the others who braved the wind and rain and dashed from the shelters along the wall to the three central buildings. "You certainly unleashed a devil of a storm."

"I didn't know," Jane said in a horrified voice. Outside the wind lashed at trees and sent branches flying across the inner courtyard. The two ships that had escaped the initial onslaught of the storm had been caught up in the surge of water and ended up running aground just south of the fortress. Little had been seen of the Adherents, and they would have to check the island carefully for any survivors after the storm blew itself out. The weather had been raging for nearly two hours with no signs of letting up. Lightening cracked constantly across the sky. They waited for another half hour and finally Jane heard the lessening of the wind, "Can't we use our maps to move the storm on?" she asked.

"Never mess with a major storm system even if you were the one to start it," Tasker muttered. "It's like trying to stop an avalanche."

Jane fell silent again and stared out the window to where the sky was slowly clearing and the clouds were no longer angry shades of green and black. When the storm finally dissipated, it was with a suddenness that left everyone staring up at the sky in awe. The curtains of rain simply stopped, and the winds died, leaving a layer of leaves and branches scattered across the fortress and the rebel forces in control of the remaining ships.

"Get a team of soldiers and go check the grounds," Tasker said to Eriunia. "Braun, if you would, take another force and search the ships. Puck and his goblins and the trolls will search the island and make sure none of the Adherents escaped."

Everyone scattered. The moment the sun began shining again a bubble of activity filled the fortress grounds. Teams of freed slaves went about clearing fallen trees and repairing damage to buildings, while the rest broke into search parties and headed to the dock or the forests.

Jane was tired, and since she had not been sent with any of the groups, she found herself wandering the outer wall of the fortress, picking up branches and hauling them out the smaller gate that led east. She soon tired of that task and began picking her way along the coast towards where a few of Puck's goblins were examining the remains of one of the Ironships.

"Is it empty?" Jane asked as she approached the small wiry fighters.

The trio looked over at her and nodded. "We think so," the tallest one muttered. "Haven't seen any movement, but Puck's order was to watch while he checks the rest of the island. So we watch."

"I'm going closer," Jane said suddenly.

This drew a round of protests from the three. "Puck said stay away," the tall one said as he turned his narrow eyes toward her.

"Well, Puck isn't here right now, is he?" Jane retorted. "I'm not a member of his forces. And I want to see it up close." She stepped onto the rocks and began to make her way toward the Ironship.

"Go get Puck," the tall goblin pushed his shortest companion, who immediately sprinted off into the forest. The tall goblin then trailed after Jane looking around nervously as they approached the ship, which was lying on its side like a beached whale.

She picked her way along the rocky shore, skirting tide pools brimming with water and debris, until she was standing next to the iron hull. The metal was cool to the touch, and when she put her hand against it, she could feel the raw, contained power. She would never have noticed this back in her own world. She saw a great gash in the side of the ship, but the surge of water that beached it had been so powerful that over half of the vessel was aground.

"Don't go inside," the goblin begged her.

"Nonsense," Jane muttered. "If there were anyone around, we would have seen something by now." The hole in the side of the ship was big enough that Jane was able to step over the jagged metal into the ship. She found herself standing on a metal walkway that seemed to be part of the steam engine area. Great pipes snaked around what looked like two huge boilers, and the heat coming from deeper inside the ship was still considerable. Rather than go further that way, Jane turned around and examined the passage that led out towards the half of the ship that was still hanging out over the water and partially submerged. The goblin beside her fingered his long hunting knife nervously as he entered the ship, his eyes darting around the darkness.

"Please, map maker, we should wait for the others," the goblin begged one last time.

"Go if you want to," Jane said with a wave of her hand. "I want to look around a little." She was feeling more adventurous today than she ever had in the past. Truthfully, she was feeling that no one thought she could fight. While others had been in danger and fought Adherents one on one, she had been in a secure place with pen and paper. She may have had a hand in winning the day, but she hadn't been one of the ones to risk bodily harm.

Jane walked down the passage, carefully ducking under the pieces of iron that had broken free on impact. The goblin waited nervously where he could see her, constantly looking back and forth. Jane shrugged. She wanted to see the ship, and she was going to explore no matter what the little creature thought. After about thirty feet she reached an intersection. A short passage led to a door on her right. She tested the latch. It opened easily, but the hinges could use some oil. When the door was finally open, she looked about the room, which was filled with crates stacked from floor to ceiling and tied down to round hooks set into the floor.

Carefully she pushed back the lid on one of the crates and looked inside. What she found inside made her blood run cold. She gasped out loud, causing the goblin to shuffle down the corridor towards her. Inside the wooden crate, carefully packed with a heavy coating of grease, were ten brand-new weapons, similar to the muskets but with parts that reminded her of the automatic weapons carried by soldiers back in her world. The barrels were twice the size of a twelve-gauge shotgun and had a wide place at the bottom where a clip could be inserted. This Cain person was upgrading his weapons. Soon his forces would not be using the old muskets but modern rifles in their conquests.

She reached out to pick up one of the rifles, when a voice spoke, and she froze.

"I wouldn't touch those."

Jane turned slowly. A dark shadow detached itself from the wall and stepped towards her. She thought about running, but the figure pointed a pistol-like weapon at her and shook his head.

"Don't try running or crying out," he said. "Try fleeing into the Divide, and I'll shoot you before you make it."

"How do you know?" Jane retorted. She tried to sound brave but her voice shook.

"Do you honestly think we haven't tested that?" he replied. "The man I shot as he was entering the Divide barely had time to scream in pain before the darkness of the Divide took him, and he was lost forever."

Jane edged back towards the crate of guns, but he shook his finger at her.

"Foolishness, girl. We stored the ammunition in a different place," he said. "Now that we have that settled, I think introductions are in order. I'm Averill. Cain sent me to deliver these weapons and deal with some issues that seem to have begun to arise around Duluth. It appears things have grown a bit worse than he thought."

"What he's doing here is evil," Jane spat back.

"So?" Averill replied. He smiled thinly. "I don't care who I work for. He pays well. I'm not one of those empty headed fools who believe in the Temple of Adherency. I'm a professional. I go where the work is."

Jane listened to his voice and knew in her heart there was little chance of convincing the man to side with the rebels. His tone was cold, and his eyes looked at her like a customer checking over a side of beef at a grocery store. No emotion was visible, just a promise that if she failed to do what he said she would die.

"Now, I have a few things that you need to do for me," Averill said coldly. "Place your map, medallion, and pen on the top of that crate. I won't turn those over to Cain. He has enough power already. Those things can stay here for your friends."

"Why would you help them?" Jane asked as she removed her map and the other items from her pockets and laid them on the wooden lid.

"I'm not helping them," Averill said with smirk. "I'm making sure Cain continues to have the need of my services for the extended future."

"I just want my sister back," Jane said dejectedly.

"Hmmm," Averill murmured as he tapped his chin. "Pretty girl with long black hair and blue eyes?"

Jane's eyes flashed angrily, "Where is she!"

Averill stepped back, the sheer fury in her voice surprised him for a moment, "She's held far from here. However, I think you'll see her sooner than you think." He motioned to the far side of the storage room where another door led out into the depths of the Ironship. "That way."

Jane looked hesitantly at her map and pen but finally followed his instructions and walked to the far door. The passage they entered ran back towards the section of the ship that was under water, and Jane was forced deeper and deeper into the ship with the cold-blooded assassin following her. Behind them they heard shouts as the rebels with Puck finally penetrated the ship and began searching for her. The passage led them into the knee-deep cold water that filled the back of the Ironship and into a cavernous hold that was home to a collection of odd looking machines.

"That one there," Averill ordered. He pointed to a long round tube machine that was mostly submerged in the water.

"Great, a submarine," Jane muttered. This was going from bad to worse for her. She waded out to where the metal hatch to the sub was open and waiting for them to enter. The machine was only about thirty feet long and about fifteen feet around, but when she climbed down the ladder the ship grew even tighter. Pipes ran everywhere inside and an odd looking engine was bolted to the center of the small deck area.

"Sit down," Averill ordered as he slid down the ladder and motioned her to the metal seat across from the pilot's chair.

Jane complied. Soon she was tied securely to the chair and listening as the engine behind them powered up.

"Here they come," Averill muttered more to himself then to his un-willing passenger. There was a loud pinging sound as shot from the magical muskets bounced off the hull of the vessel. Averill didn't seem concerned.

Jane felt the sudden drop as Averill reached up and pulled a long lever attached to the ceiling. A second surge of power, and the propeller bit into the water and pushed them towards the hull of the Ironship. She could not see how he planned on exiting the vessel but her unasked question was answered when he tapped a big red button on the controls before him. Seconds later, the gates exploded outwards in a flash of fire and torn metal.

"Where are you taking me?" Jane demanded as they surged free of the ruined ship and began to sink below the waves.

"To see your beloved sister," Averill said with a laugh. "That's what you wanted, wasn't it? Of course, without you, this minor rebellion will fade, and I'll finally take my revenge against the little dwarf. Oh, yes, I know who came to you and begged you to help him. Rest assured that there's a lot about Tasker you don't know. The mouthpiece of god he called himself when he started his Temple. Thrown out of every city in the old world, he finally came here. He even tried to take over Ireland at one point and was firmly shown the way to leave. Then he found Cain and recognized a popular leader when he saw him, so he trained him in the ways of map making and started using him to gain converts here in the new world. Ah, but before he knew what was happening, Cain took over and started making real changes. Tasker, he got cold feet then, tried to part ways." Averill laughed. "When you join the Temple you join for life."

Jane sat silently wondering if she really knew anything at all about the small dwarf Tasker, it seemed each time she met someone outside the rebellion she was finding out new bits of the story behind him. Or it could be the assassin was lying to her. Either way, she was stuck.

"But what does that have to do with me, you ask?" Averill said as he touched the throttle next to the captain's chair and sent them surging forward through the water.

Jane listened as she watched the great curved window in front of them. Fish scattered as the submarine rocketed through the water, and Averill deftly guided them past towering rock formations. The water this far from shore was still clean and visibility was good. Jane even thought she saw a startled but very human looking face looking back at her at one point. A large compass was built into the control panel, and Jane watched the needle swing around until they were powering north.

"Where are you taking me?" Jane asked finally when she decided that he would not volunteer the information.

"North," Averill said cryptically. She already knew that much.

"The Isle of Lakes?" Jane said taking a shot in the dark. She must have been right because she saw his eyes widen momentarily before his control re-asserted itself.

"Perhaps," Averill replied.

Jane sighed and leaned back, trying to place her body in a more comfortable position. It would most likely be a long ride and she saw little chance of her escaping until they arrived. Without her map and anchor she was stuck, thankfully he had not searched her and the compass remained tucked inside the deepest pocket of her jacket.

"By all means, get comfortable. We'll be there in eight hours," Averill said almost to himself. He slid his own seat into a more comfortable position and leaned to rest his eyes. "Don't worry. This ship moves faster than anything afloat and carries ten explosive charges that can take down even the biggest of the Ironships."

Jane's face paled as his words sank in. They had captured their Ironships and planned on using them to take back the lands around Lake Superior, but the Adherents already possessed the ability to sink their entire captured flotilla.

"I see you understand," Averill said quietly. "Yes, I know you've taken several Ironships stationed at Madeline Isle. It'll gain you nothing. This one small vessel already possesses the power to sink every ship you can float. It's pointless, Jane. Tasker can't win." He turned away from her and focused on the controls that guided the submarine through the crystal water of the deep parts of Lake Superior.

Jane leaned back, trying to keep from moving. The ropes were tight but not enough to cut off the circulation in her arms, so she wiggled into a comfortable position and settled in for the trip. Hours passed. Jane dozed once, awakening when the submarine rose out of the water. A grand expanse filled her eyes. This side of Isle Royal was filled with industrial buildings and black smoke belched out, hiding the sun.

"What are you doing to this world?" Jane whispered.

Averill did not respond as he guided the submarine along the surface towards a great bay that filled this side of the island. The natural peninsula that protected the bay had been built up with great granite stones and two more lighthouses had been added to mark the extended water break. The Isle Royal Lighthouse Jane had seen once in a picture seemed to look the same but the old brick house once attached to the structure was gone. In its place she saw a thick-walled fortress that bristled with cannons. Above the structure a flag waved in the wind. A blood-red background provided the backdrop for a fist and forearm that pointed down as though smashing something to the ground. Above the fist were two words in a language Jane couldn't read. She asked Averill what they said.

"Science and Magic," he replied. "That was Tasker's thought when he started his Temple. He wanted to bring the science of your world here to our side of the Divide, claiming he'd make life easier. Some thought differently. They said the old ways were best. That's why he was asked to leave the Council."

In front of them the docking berths of the great Ironships stretched out as far as Jane could see from their current position. They slowly cruised the length of the docks, and Jane counted twenty warships sitting peacefully in their berths. Crewmen and soldiers crawled all over the ships, readying them for war. At the innermost parts of the great docking facility, another sight that drew her attention.

Jane stared in awe at the massive behemoth sitting in a tremendous dry dock. Hundreds of workers swarmed over the hull. The ship itself seemed to be complete. It was double the size of any other Ironship afloat. As they glided by, she saw cannon after cannon being loaded. Then Averill pulled the submarine into a small berth at the innermost part of the shipyard.

"Welcome to the Isle of Lakes," Averill said as he untied the ropes holding her to the metal chair, and then motioned for her to stand. "Shall we go ashore?"

CHAPTER THIRTEEN

The Rebellion Falters

Noon or so

TASKER WAS IN A FRENZY. Jane was missing, and the last person to see her was a goblin who reported that she had entered the grounded Ironship south of the fortress. They had searched what parts of the ship they could reach and found no sign of her, but an explosion had been reported soon after she disappeared, and Tasker was forced to assume she was dead in the depths of the ship.

"What do we do?" Eriunia asked as she stepped out of the hulking remains of the ship and looked to where Tasker was sitting on the beach with his head in his hands.

"What difference does it make?" Tasker muttered. "Without a Map Maker to counter Cain's powers, what chance do we have?" The dwarf waved his hand in a helpless gesture and returned to staring at the ground between his feet.

"Move the weapons to the fortress," Eriunia said to Braun as she turned away from the dwarf. His will to fight this day was gone. She would have to deal with him later. The elves were involved in this struggle, even if they didn't want to be, and she wouldn't let the rebels' hard-won gains disappear because one dwarf was feeling sorry for himself. "And find the ammunition for them. Those new guns are years ahead of the magic muskets. If we use them at the right time they'll change the course of at least one battle."

There were nods among the gathered rebels and a long line formed, passing the heavy crates out of the depths of the ship and stacking them on the rocks. When the ship had been ransacked completely the mound of supplies covered an area almost fifty feet long and twenty feet wide.

Sometime during the work, Tasker had disappeared and left Braun to oversee the hauling of the supplies back to the fortress. When the last of the crates had disappeared up the coast and the ship thoroughly checked one last time, the goblins surrounded the ship started digging. Braun watched for a time as the goblins put their natural tunneling skills to use and removed great sections of stone and earth. Slowly the ship righted itself and settled into the depression they'd dug in the ground. When they completed their efforts, the Ironship was upright and the hull held firmly in the ground. The gaping holes and the crumpled underwater doors were clear and ready to be repaired when supplies were found.

"What do we do about Tasker?" Braun said as he walked with Eriunia towards the distant fortress.

"Give him some time," Eriunia replied. "He feels much guilt for what's happened over the last century. His goals when he started his movement were not all bad, if just a bit misguided. Now it seems his chance to set things right and relieve the suffering he caused is slipping away again."

"Do you really think Jane's dead?" Braun asked. He hadn't known the girl long, and her part in all their effort didn't seem as grand as Tasker thought it was intended to be.

"It's hard to tell," Eriunia said as she skirted a rough boulder. "We found nothing inside the ship but the gaping hole in the back. It was blown outward, though, not inward. It couldn't have happened by an impact with the shore. Something forced its way out of the ship. She may have been taken captive and is still alive. The fact that we found her map and pen and anchor attests to that."

"She's on her way to Cain's grip, then," Braun interjected.

"That's possible," Eriunia agreed. "But look around you. The Prison Isles are prisons no longer, the Lake Huron Fleet is now missing fully half of its strength, and we have at least three Ironships under our control and two more if we can find the supplies to fix them. That doesn't include the cargo carriers, which can be used to land troops wherever we strike next."

"You intend to carry this through to the end, don't you?" Braun asked as he stopped and looked at her. "It was your father's wish that you return to Tuatha De Danann and be safe."

"My father has forgotten I was taken from the safety of the elvish retreat with little trouble," Eriunia shot back. "Someone opened the gate for Cain's Adherents to enter our safety, and Cain has already converted people among the elvish race who long for a return to this world and for power here on earth. The elvish race is not immune to his message of power and glory. He has led many astray with that siren's call."

Braun lowered his eyes and found he could not disagree with her. He knew what was in his own heart. At times what he saw there made him ashamed.

"What is it Braun?" Eriunia said when she saw the normally proud elf seemingly warring with his own emotions.

"Nothing," Braun replied. He forced away the dark thoughts and focused on task at hand. He'd deal with his own orders from the king later. Now was not the time or the place.

They arrived back at the fortress to a hubbub of commotion and shouts of different people trying to be heard.

"What's going on?" Eriunia asked a nearby dwarf rebel whose face was scarred from beatings taken from the Adherents.

"We captured an Adherent," he said with a laugh. "He's the captain of one of the Ironships that sank during the storm. Tasker's going to hang him from the tower."

"That fool!" Eriunia burst out. "Braun, go gather some of the more level-headed fighters we can trust and meet me there." She didn't wait to see if he would follow her instructions but rushed off towards the main gate across from the small gate leading south. Already a crowd had gathered, laughing and urging on the proceedings above them. Tasker had already looped a thick rope around an iron ring set in the stone used for holding torches. He was in the process of tying the noose around the bedraggled Adherent's neck. A wild and unhinged look was in Tasker's eyes, and his hands trembled as they tried to tie the knot.

"Tasker!" Eriunia shouted, but her voice was lost among the crowd around her. She needed to get closer for him to hear her. She pushed through the packed bodies until she was standing below the gate surrounded by at least four or five hundred rebels. Everyone shouted and chanted insults at the frightened Adherent, then, from somewhere in the crowd, a small pistol shot rang out. A projectile struck the ship's captain in the leg, and he nearly buckled. Eriunia shouted again, but still her voice was but one of many. The heat of the bodies surrounded her and their anger rolled over her until she could stand it no longer. Suddenly the power of her ancestors burst out from her and rolled out in a wave of power that brought a starlted, sudden silence.

"TASKER!" Eriunia shouted, her voice the only one that spoke. Those around her shrank back in fear as the bared power of an elvish princess was released.

"What!" Tasker responded, his voice filled with barely contained rage.

"Stop this farce immediately," Eriunia said in a level tone and punctuated each word with a small crack of lightening that sent sparks cascading across the paving stones.

"No," Tasker replied. "His kind has pillaged and plundered our lands and people for too long. No more!" There was a muttering of agreement from those gathered.

"So we will use the same tactics against them they have employed against us and become the same thing we now fight?" Eriunia reasoned aloud. "Will we kill and torture our way through every city that dares to resist us? Is that what we should do? Shall we start with Duluth?" The bloodlust of the crowd was beginning to wane, and slowly the crowd's thirst for vengeance faded as cooler heads began thinking once again.

Tasker looked around. His mind began to clear, and the rope in his hand slowly slipped to the ground. He watched as Eriunia mounted the steps and walked to where he stood with the Adherent captain.

"Lock him in one of the cells," Eriunia ordered.

The soldiers nodded and escorted the frightened man through the now silent crowd and away from the waiting noose. When they were out of sight, she turned back to Tasker and put her hand on his shoulder. There were tears in his eyes when he looked up at her and finally spoke.

"I started all this," Tasker said quietly. "The deaths, the horrors that have happened . . . they're all on my shoulders."

"No, old friend, they're not," Eriunia replied. "You tried to start something to improve people's lives and made some mistakes on the way. This world was stagnant. Many of its rulers were corrupt, but what Cain did to you was wrong. He twisted your goals of bringing new science to this world and made it into something you knew was wrong. No one's worked harder against what he's doing than you have. We all know that judgment is coming someday for what we've done with our time here. I think that, when the creator judges you, he'll take your actions into account and the fact that you've been trying to right those actions."

Tasker looked up at her, and a new determination filled his face, "You're right. I think that's why the elvish people made their refuge so long ago—to avoid the foolish whims of the rest of us." Tasker wiped away the bit of moisture that had crept up into his eyes, and he felt as though a fog was clearing from his mind. An alertness he had not felt in days came back to him. He looked about, wondering if the Adherents had managed to place someone close to him. The feelings that had affected him over the last few days seemed out of place. He waved to those gathered in the courtyard, "Go. Prepare yourself for the coming days. Our battle is not finished in any way."

"Now, shall we go speak to the captain you nearly hung?" Eriunia asked. "He may have some important information for us. We haven't captured anyone so high up in their organization until now."

"Aye," Tasker muttered. "A better plan then where I was headed only moments ago." He smiled at her sheepishly and followed her down the steps to where Braun and his soldiers were getting the crowd moving again in more constructive ways. There was food to prepare, supplies to be stored, and ammunition for the weapons to find and distribute.

Tasker and Eriunia crossed the courtyard and entered the block house where the Adherent had been placed into a holding cell and approached the man. He was seated on the stones at the back of the cell and looked up hopefully as they approached, but fear filled his face when Tasker entered. *This is something they can use,* thought Eriunia, as she followed Tasker into the cell. She stepped forward to take the lead and hoped Tasker would follow her.

"We cannot just kill him, Tasker," Eriunia said loudly as though trying to convince the dwarf of something.

"What?" Tasker said but he quickly caught on to her meaning and his role. "And why not?" he growled and pulled a dagger from his belt. He examined the blade as if assessing its sharpness. "We are rebels after all. They've killed so many of our people. You may have fooled those outside, but you can't fool me, elf." Tasker stepped forward with a gleam in his eyes. "I'm going to cut his throat from ear to ear."

"Soon, my friend, soon. Right now, he can still be of use to us," Eriunia said, and watched as horror blossomed in the man's face. She stepped between the seemingly blood-thirsty dwarf and his target. "Give me a chance at least to try to convince him to help us." She turned to the Adherent captain and said, "Don't move too quickly. I'm not sure how long I can keep him from harming you."

"Look, I never wanted anything to do with the Temple," the Adherent said. "It was join them or see my family hauled off to the mines." He looked around nervously as two burly human fighters entered the cell. Then Braun slipped in and glared at him.

"I'm sure that's the case, but my friends here have been severely mistreated by people wearing the same robes you now wear," Eriunia explained. "They want revenge, and right now the only thing stopping them from taking it is the hope that you can tell us why the Lake Huron fleet was steaming here and what you were carrying."

"We had no idea anything was happening on the Prison . . . I mean here on Madeline Island," he stammered. "This was a routine training mission and delivery of . . ." he licked his dry lips nervously. "Please, if I betray Cain, he'll have me and my whole family killed." He broke down and tears flowed freely from his eyes. "I have a wife and three children living on Manitoulin Island under the thumbs of the Temple priests."

"Well, sadly for you, if you don't tell us what Tasker wants to know you'll probably never see any of them ever again," Eriunia said as she looked back to where Tasker was edging closer, his dagger ready. His face was locked into a fierce scowl, and his fingers twitched nervously.

Keeping an eye on Tasker, the Adherent said, "Look, Cain's managed to bring back several advanced versions of muskets from across the Divide. It's taken them years to discover how to make them work on our side, but he finally managed it. The *Black Dawn* was carrying crates of the new type of weapon. The ammunition was shipped on one of the other ships. I think it was the *Moon Dust*."

"Where's the *Moon Dust*?" Eriunia asked curiously.

"It was one of the first ships to dock this morning," the captain responded. "I think it sank when you opened fire on the docked vessels."

Eriunia motioned to Braun and he nodded.

When the elf was gone, she turned back to the Adherent. "What else were you carrying?" she asked.

"Nothing, ma'am," he insisted.

His face was pale, and he licked his lips nervously, telling Eriunia that indeed there was more to his story, but she was running short on time. She stepped aside and said, "Fine, Tasker. He's all yours. Try not to kill him too quickly. Maybe we can get the rest of the story from him once he feels a little pain." She turned away in disinterest. "After all, he's just a human. There are plenty more of those around." The tone of her voice was cold as if she was discussing the death of a flea or a cockroach.

Tasker smiled and stalked towards the captain, his knife held low. "I'm going to gut him. That's always a nice, slow, painful death. After all, my own family died by an Adherent's hand. Why shouldn't he die slowly, knowing his wife and children will never see him again?"

"No, wait!" the Adherent cried. "One of the other ships was carrying something, something meant to patrol Lake Superior in case someone managed to capture an Ironship." He scrambled backwards, but the rebel guards grabbed him and restrained him so Tasker could move in nice and close. "I didn't see it, but I heard about it. They said it was a ship that could go under the water and fire its weapons unseen from the surface. There were also rumors Cain was having something really special built at the Isle of Lakes. A ship meant to spearhead his attack when the Divide falls, but I don't know what it is. Please don't kill me." He pleaded as Tasker's face came to within an inch of his own face.

"Why not?" Tasker growled. No longer playing at his anger, he was itching to send this filthy Adherent into the afterlife to be judged.

"Please, I told you everything I could," the captain blubbered. "I just want to see my Marie again, and my babies, my precious babies."

Tasker stopped and shook his head. He couldn't kill someone like this. Eriunia was right. He really wasn't a cold-blooded killer. If they were to succeed, they'd have to take a better road then Adherents. They would not stoop to their level.

"That was why the back of the grounded Ironship was blown outwards," Eriunia reasoned. She looked at Tasker. "You know what that means. Someone made it out of the ship soon after she entered."

"The vessel escaped?" the captain said. "That means *he* escaped."

"Who?" Tasker asked curiously.

"One of *them* was onboard," the captain said with a shudder. "Hired killers from the old world, bronzed skin and dark hair. They send their assassins out of the hidden fortress and leave daggers as calling cards when they kill." He was nearly whispering. "You can't see them when they come for you. All you feel is the cold iron as it enters and takes the life from you. Please don't leave me alone. If Cain finds out I spoke to you, he'll send one of them after me." The Adherent captain completely broke down and had to be restrained as he tried to flee, the terror on his face very real.

"Chain him to the wall," Tasker ordered. "We need to talk." He motioned for Eriunia to follow him out the door while the burly rebels fastened chains around the Adherent's arms and locked him securely to the stone wall.

Once outside the cell and with the door securely shut, Tasker turned to Eriunia, "You know what he was talking about, don't you?" he said. "We've never seen one of their kind here in the new world. Cain's power must truly be growing if he was able to afford to hire the Brotherhood to oversee his intelligence efforts."

"This complicates things," Eriunia agreed. "I must tell Braun. He's one of the few elves outside our refuge who can match blades with a Brotherhood assassin."

"If he took Jane and the underwater vessel, he's most likely making for the Isle of Lakes," Tasker reasoned. "Twenty ships there against our four. We can't attack by sea. But where brute force fails, maybe subterfuge can succeed." He motioned for Eriunia to follow him, and they walked to the end of the passage where they could be alone. Slowly as the evening came and deepened, a plan began to take shape. By night they were making arrangements that would either bring them safely through the Isle of Lakes or leave them rotting in the deepest of Cain's many dungeons.

CHAPTER FOURTEEN

Bella's Troubles

Evening

J ACOB SLEPT PEACEFULLY, and his body regained its spent energy. When he awoke, the sun was setting behind the surrounding mountains. Flying Cloud was awake and standing near the small lake. Yerdarva had emerged from her lair and was standing across the lake from them facing the broad opening that led into the heart of the mountain.

"How are you?" Flying Cloud asked and smiled at Jacob.

He smiled back and shrugged, "Feeling better than I was before. Where's Bella?"

"She went to report to Tasker," Flying Cloud said. "We're going to make the trip with Yerdarva." She tucked her arm into Jacob's and edged closer as a chill wind kicked up waves on the lake before them. "Burr, it's getting cold."

Jacob hesitated a moment, then put his arm around her and pulled her a bit closer. He used his arm to flip his cloak around both of them. The dragon was doing something in front of her cavern. Suddenly the ground shook. She moved away as a great avalanche of boulders cascaded down the mountainside. The opening to her lair disappeared under a pile of stone.

"What's she doing?" Jacob asked. He tried to focus on the dragon but found himself more interested in the young woman beside him.

"She's sealing her cavern for now," Flying Cloud explained. "Watch." She pointed. The dragon had loosed a belch of dragon's fire against the stones. Moments later the mass of boulders fused together into a solid mess of iron and stone. "Any creature would be hard pressed to break through that mixture of iron and stone. Her egg should be safe."

Jacob looked with awe as the dragon loosed several more blasts of fire against the mountainside and sealed away her cavern. When she seemed satisfied, she turned and rounded the lake with great leaping bounds that brought her to them.

"In the morning we'll head east before the sun rises," Yerdarva said, her voice a rumble of anger, and her eyes narrowed to mere slits. "Tonight I will hunt and eat my fill." She leapt into the air, and the sound of wings flapping filled the night. Then silence descended once again.

Jacob and Flying Cloud stood talking for almost an hour near the shore when a sound drew their attention. Jacob turned to see the mushroom ring circling wildly, the lights dancing around and around. Then Bella erupted from the portal and fell limply to the ground. She seemed exhausted. Jacob and Flying Cloud rushed to her side.

"What happened?" Flying Cloud asked as she carefully picked up the limp fairy and cradled her in her own arms. The fairy was panting in exhaustion, and her small body was covered with cuts and bruises.

"A Brotherhood assassin was waiting inside the mushroom circle near Duluth," Bella panted. She shivered. "It's cold here," she whispered.

Jacob grabbed the corner of a warm blanket and cut a section of it for the fairy, carefully wrapping it around her. Then he noticed one of Bella's wings was badly ripped, and small drops of blood spilled to the ground.

"Her wings," Jacob whispered to Flying Cloud. "Can you help her heal?" His heart beat wildly in concern as Flying Cloud turned Bella onto her side and looked in horror at the torn wing.

"I don't know," Flying Cloud whispered. "Hold her while I get some things from my bandolier bag. We must move quickly before she loses any more blood." Carefully she wrapped the blanket so that it would not touch the torn wing, then handed Bella's limp form to Jacob.

"I got lost on the way back and jumped out at Duluth to get my bearings," Bella murmured. She seemed beyond pain, and her eyes were glassy. "He was on me in a rush, but I managed to stick him once with an arrow. His knife caught my wing as I went back into the circle . . ." She paused a moment and coughed. "Almost didn't find my way back . . ."

"Hold her steady," Flying Cloud said as she crouched down to where Jacob cradled the fairy. "We have to stop the bleeding." She held her medicine bag tightly in her hand. She produced a small vial of liquid and poured a small amount into her hand. Carefully she allowed the fragrant oil to touch the wounds. Almost immediately the bleeding stopped. She then reached inside her bandolier bag and pulled out a small crystal.

Jacob cradled Bella's limp form, while Flying Cloud prayed desperately and carefully placed the crystal against the torn parts of Bella's wing. With the flow of blood already stopped, she focused on the wing. As she examined it, she saw the wing was torn almost completely from Bella's back. Carefully she passed the crystal over the fragile, torn membranes, hoping that the crystal's magic would bring the torn flesh back together.

Jacob's arms cramped from holding Bella still, and for a while he was not even sure he could still see her chest moving up and down, but after some time she coughed weakly. Her eyes fluttered open, and she smiled slightly at him.

"I think she's going to make it," Jacob said to Flying Cloud.

"I'm glad," Flying Cloud said weakly. Exhausted, she swayed on her feet, nearly collapsing into the embers that still remained of their campfire.

Jacob managed to free one of his hands and carefully guided Flying Cloud down to the ground next to him. He sat down with his back against a moss-covered tree and managed to tip a log onto the fire with his foot. Next to him, Flying Cloud pulled a blanket up around herself and half across him before she fell into an exhausted sleep with her head resting on his left arm. In his right arm, curled almost into a tiny ball, Bella slept peacefully, her mangled wing limp against her back. It was back in one piece but had not moved once.

Jacob dozed off and on, awaking with a start when Yerdarva returned from her hunt. The dragon looked satisfied and blood dripped from her jaws.

"What happened?" the dragon asked as she walked daintily into the campsite and lay her massive body down next to the fire.

"Bella lost her way and came out of a mushroom circle near Duluth," Jacob said quietly as he tried to restore feeling to his arms without waking either of the sleeping figures. "She said a Brotherhood assassin was waiting for her and cut her with a knife as she was trying to escape."

Yerdarva shook her head sadly. "The Brotherhood is an evil organization steeped in dark power. If they're now employed by Cain, that's a bad sign. They're masters of the art of moving in the shadows and killing in silence. They're as cunning as vipers and deadly as cobras." The dragon looked down with pity on the tiny fairy. "She's lucky to have survived the attack and made it back to us."

"They need sleep," Jacob said softly as he looked down at the slumbering figures.

"We'll stay here tonight and leave in the morning," Yerdarva said. "Rest, Jacob. I'll watch over your sleep. Tomorrow at first light we'll move."

* * * * *

JACOB AWOKE THE NEXT MORNING with a start as the memories of the night before flooded back to him. His arms were both stiff, but Bella was still sleeping quietly wrapped in a corner of the blanket and Flying Cloud was moving slowly about the camp watching over a pan filled with sizzling potatoes and strips of venison.

"Will she be able to fly again?" Jacob asked softly.

Flying Cloud frowned. "I do not know. The wing was torn so badly, and I'm not the healer my grandpa is." She carefully took the pan from the fire and dished out portions for each of them. Down by the lake, Yerdarva was sipping water. Now and then she'd flip her head back and send a fish slipping down her long throat.

Jacob sat up. The movement roused Bella, who sat up slowly and craned her head around to look at her wing.

"I can't feel it at all," Bella said quietly. Her face showed strain as she tried to move the appendage and failed. She stretched out her feet to the ground as Jacob leaned over and set her down. After a moment her balance returned, and she was able to walk without aid, but the injured wing refused to move. It hung limply at her back even as the other wing beat the air furiously.

"I'll carry her," Yerdarva said as she returned from the lake. She fastened a rough harness to her upper back with straps that stretched back to where they would sit.

Jacob and Flying Cloud ate quickly and then kicked dirt over the fire until it was completely out. After gathering what supplies they could carry, they climbed onto the dragon's broad back. Bella sat before them on the dragon's powerful shoulders while they got settled.

"Hang on tightly," Yerdarva said over her shoulder. "The take-off can be a bit rough," She warned. The dragon gave two great bounding leaps and worked her wings in strong strokes that sent them rocketing into the air and forced Jacob and Flying Cloud to hang on for dear life. Bella had not stayed on the dragon's shoulders, but was tucked inside Jacob's cloak and clung to him tightly.

"How long will it take us to get there?" Jacob called out over the rush of wind. They were circling the lake as the dragon gained altitude. Finally she banked away from the mountain and began streaking over the forest of pines that covered the lands below the mountains.

"Much of the day," Yerdarva called back as she headed east across the mountains. It was chilly this high up. Despite the sun, the air's chill left them shivering. "We'll pass over the Isle of Lakes. I plan to give the Adherents something to think about besides what Tasker and the others are up to."

"We know Jane's sister's being held there," Jacob said loudly. "Maybe the two of us can sneak in and free her while you provide a distraction."

"Oh, I'll be doing a bit more than distracting them," Yerdarva growled. Bits of smoke puffed from her mouth as she rocketed over the hills and vales. She weaved deftly through passages between mountains and dipped down in valleys unseen. They worked their way east and south stopping only once at the Bighorn Mountains while the great dragon killed several mountain sheep and ate them in great rending bites.

Jacob turned away while the dragon ate. It wasn't the blood that bothered him, but the flashing of her massive teeth. They made him nervous. When her hunger was sated they remounted the dragon and were off again, soaring over the wide expanses of what would have been North Dakota. Later in the afternoon they passed over a small encampment that hugged the banks of the Red River and began flying over the forests that covered Minnesota. It was odd for Jacob to see the state in such a pristine condition—no highways or power lines cris-crossing the landscape. The rolling hills and forests were broken only by expanses of deep blue water, trademarks of the land of ten thousand lakes.

"We'll be there soon," Yerdarva called to them as she flew lower and lower. Finally the first view of Lake Superior blossomed before them, and the first signs of civilization appeared. Ruined cottages and collapsed walls marked the remains of a village that hugged the granite cliffs of the North Shore. A few miles north of their position they saw the smoky cloud that covered the Isle of Lakes and the great shipyards that filled the industrial city built by Cain.

"Three hours till sunset," Jacob muttered as he looked at his watch. "It's six in the evening. We need to get a little closer and find a way into the city."

Yerdarva ran along the coasts bringing them, as close as she could to their destination just as the sun began to set. Finally they soared down behind a hill that blocked their view of the island. The dragon landed and motioned for them to dismount.

"You must find a way to enter the city and see if you can free Jackie. I'm going to burn the outer guard posts and draw their attention to me," the dragon said. "I'll start at midnight even if you're not in place. Good hunting to you." Her voice seemed sad and her eyes even more so.

"We'll see you again," Jacob said hopefully.

"I don't know, young Runner," Yerdarva replied. "Cain has many powerful weapons at his disposal, some of them strong enough even to slay a full-grown dragon such as myself." She stopped for a moment and then continued. "I truly hope to see you again, but if not in this lifetime then perhaps in the afterlife."

"What of your egg?" Jacob asked.

"He has hatched and has ample food," Yerdarva said with a touch of pride. "It was my last act as his mother. He will be safe inside the mountain until I either return to break the protections or break them himself when he is strong enough." She turned her head and pulled her lips back in an imitation of a smile.

Jacob put one hand on the noble creature's neck and patted it sadly. She seemed resigned to the idea that she would not survive the coming battle. "I'm not going to say good bye, just see you soon."

Yerdarva nodded and then leaped into the air and disappeared to the west. She hunted one last time to fill her strength and prepare for the battle coming that night.

CHAPTER FIFTEEN

The Ferry Crossing

Evening

J ACOB AND FLYING CLOUD followed a narrow trail leading to the lake shore, with Bella sitting on Jacob's shoulder. Despite the massive collection of stone and timber buildings covering the distant shores of the Isle of Lakes, the nearby shore of Lake Superior was home to a simple dock and a tattered ferry. Three timber huts clustered around the dock, and four men stood nearby talking when they approached.

Jacob squared his shoulders and wore his anchor prominently on his chest. Bella wore a small collar around her neck, and a thin piece of leather that looked like a leash stretched to Flying Clouds hand. They had discussed the best options, and Jacob decided to approach boldly with his anchor out hoping that the lesser Adherents would be cowed by his supposed status.

"Who are you?"

Jacob turned his best arrogant sneer to the man and glared at him, "Get the ferry ready to cross." He continued towards the rickety boat tied to the short dock. The boat was about thirty feet long and wallowed awkwardly on the waves.

"But we are done for the night," complained one of the men.

Jacob whirled and drew his sword from its sheath, resting the blade moments later on the man's neck. "I have business in the city. I will not be slowed down, even if I need to bury some of you."

The rough looking boatman stumbled back as his face paled. He glanced at his friends and then hurried towards the ferry. "Come on. Let's get this over with." The ferry man's voice shook as he ordered his fellow workers to ready the vessel for travel.

The sun was disappearing in the west as they pulled away from the dock. The lake surface calmed as the sun set, and the men slowly pulled with the oars, hoping for a favorable wind to speed up the journey.

"Sun's almost gone."

"What matter?" Jacob replied evenly to the master of the ferry. He turned a cold look on the man and waited for him to continue.

"It's just that weird things happen in the open water after dark."

Jacob let out an exasperated hiss. "Fine. Drop us on this side of the island," Jacob replied shortly. Already they were half way to the Isle of Lakes and the last purple clouds were vanishing from the sky. Around them the water had gone calm, as if the lake was holding its breath and waiting to see what the night might bring.

"Yes, sir," the ferry man nodded.

Another hour passed and the island slowly grew closer until they had come within a hundred yards of the city. The shore on this side of the island were covered with stone dwellings and smaller docks, the homes of fishermen with smaller vessels.

"Where do you want us to dock?" the ferry man asked.

Jacob looked at the man and noticed he wasn't as nervous as he had been earlier. *They're planning something*, he thought. He waited to answer and noticed several of the men looked at Flying Cloud with open lust. They wanted the woman and Bella and would do anything to have them, especially now that they felt closer to their own base of power.

"Any of the smaller docks," Jacob motioned with a wave of his hand. He turned slightly and used the motion to place his hand on his sword hilt. "Get ready," he intoned to Flying Cloud. As the ferry captain turned away, Jacob pulled his shield from his back and slipped his arm into the straps. About twenty feet of space separated them from the dock when the ferry master decided to make his move.

On shore, nothing moved as darkness settled fully across the island, Jacob heard the rush of footsteps and pulled his sword from its sheath, whipping around and swinging a wide blow that made all the men falter. He slammed the nearest oarsman across the head with his shield, sending him to the deck. From Flying Cloud's shoulder Bella's tiny bow hummed, and another man reeled backwards, an arrow sticking from his throat.

"Get them, boys!" the ferry master shouted breaking the silence.

Suddenly there was a wash of light across the ferry. Everyone stopped to look towards shore. A dark shape swooped out of the sky and a line of dragon's fire engulfed the buildings clustered near the dock where the ferry normally sat. Yerdarva's massive wings rocked across the open water. She spit a line of fire over the smaller dwellings just north of them. Moments later the dragon was gone north, and Jacob grabbed Flying Cloud's hand and picked up Bella. He leapt for the dock. They tumbled to the wooden planks as the ferry crashed into the rocks near shore with a grinding sound as the hull gave way under the sharp rocks.

Jacob led them up the dock and away from the shouts of the ferry men. North of where they stood the sickly glow of flames sprouted from the wooden building as the dragon scortched everything.

"We need to find out where the prisoners are held," Jacob muttered. The city around them filled with chaos, every creature and man ran to the streets and streamed north to answer the tolling of the fire warning bells.

"Rumor says that the dungeons below the Viscount's castle are filled with prisoners," Bella muttered as she clung to Jacob's shoulder. "We would have to find a way into the castle." She pointed east and north where a series of blocky towers rose into the night sky.

"That's where we'll start then," Jacob replied. He shouldered his way into the crowd with Flying Cloud clinging to him and started towards the fortress.

* * * * *

Earlier the same day

ERIUNIA AND TASKER HAD rested very little after arriving at the mushroom circle just north of the Isle of Lakes. Up the shore from where they stood was a rough collection of buildings that surrounded the docks where the cargo ships carrying iron loaded and traveled throughout the Great Lakes. Filtering through the forest behind them came most of Puck's goblins and almost two-hundred of the best warriors their small rebellion could find.

"We need to take the cargo docks quietly," Tasker whispered one last time. "No one can escape. If word gets out, they'll send out the army stationed on the Isle of Lakes, and we'll have to run."

Those gathered around him nodded. The beginning of the plan was simple enough—take the docks and continue to operate them as if nothing had happened. Rebels were dressed as Adherents and would operate all the key points while the goblins ranged through the forests, acting as scouts. Then a small party would stow away aboard one of the cargo ships in route to the Isle of Lakes and attempt to infiltrate the dungeons under the castle.

Tasker waited until he received word that the net of scouts was in place and then he led his force through the forest towards the docks. Four great buildings were arranged about the two long docks that stretched out into the lake. Around the four buildings was a scattered collection of small log dwellings and a pair of watch towers. Those watch towers had to be taken, and they had to be taken quickly. Luckily, the watchers atop the towers seemed more interested in the line of ore wagons rattling down the dirt road from the north.

"Go," Tasker motioned Braun, and two elf warriors forward. The lithe fighters dashed out of the cover of the trees and sprinted across the hundred yards of open ground that separated them from the first tower. Tasker and Eriunia held their breath until the three were standing with their backs to the wooden structure. The tower was closed on all sides, and a thick oaken door guarded the stairs leading to the top. They saw Braun bend over the lock for a moment. A few minutes later the lock fell away and the three elves disappeared into the depths of the watch tower.

"They're in," Tasker said. He motioned to the rebels crouched in the forest behind him. "Let's go. Remember no one can get away to raise the warning." With those words he led his force from the trees, but quickly heard a startled shout from the nearest watch tower, but it was cut quickly. With a flash of knife blades, Braun and the others entered the top of the tower and made short work of the unsuspecting Adherents.

The battle to overrun the docks went quickly, with some confused shouts but very few fights. Three Adherents in the second watch tower managed to fire their muskets once before Braun picked the iron lock and overwhelm them. Tasker led fully half the rebel force across the docks, where two cargo ships were tied off to the wooden structure and the crews offered no resistance as the grim-faced rebels leapt over the railings and restrained them.

"What do we do with the crews?" a rebel asked.

"Lock them in a warehouse and keep a close watch on them," Tasker ordered as the prisoners marched down the dock. Two buildings were filled with stalls, and empty wagons waited to return to the iron mines. One of the buildings was completely empty but showed signs of having recently been used to house cattle. The last one was filled with iron ore waiting to be loaded into the ships. "You know what to do," Tasker said, nodding to the bearded rebel in an Adherent's robe and toting a magical musket.

"We'll keep things running and make no noise," he confirmed. "We'll force a few of the captives to show us their standard routines ..." he held up his hands. "Don't worry we won't hurt anyone too badly," he said with a smile. "Nothing permanent anyway." His big toothy grin made Tasker chuckle before he turned to where Braun hand-picked the lock and forced his way aboard the fully loaded ship.

"Are we ready?" Tasker asked.

"Aye, the captain claimed this ship was heading to the Isle of Lakes," Braun replied. "He claims they've been dropping iron there for the last few months. Says the shipyard there is working on something."

"Did he say what?" Tasker asked.

"Nay, claimed he didn't know," Braun replied. "Claims the yard workers have been very close lipped about the whole thing."

"Well, there's little we can do about it right now," Tasker said. The last of his small group boarded the ship, an iron-hulled vessel similar in design to the Ironships that prowled the Great Lakes to protect the iron trade but without cannons or defenses. It was simply a great iron hull with rough crews quarters and a steam room that harnessed the earth's magnetic lines to drive a propeller and a simple steering mechanism.

"The cargo hold's about half full," Braun reported. "Hopefully it is enough to keep the watchers on the Isle from suspecting anything more than incompetence at play here."

"Good," Tasker replied. It was already well past midday and they still had a two hour journey by ship to reach the far side of the Isle of Lakes and carry out the rest of their plan.

* * * * *

Present day

IT WAS ANOTHER WEEK until Jackie saw Carvin again. This time he slipped inside the door and motioned for her to be quiet. He stood at the door listening for almost a full minute before turning and walking to where she was waiting.

"Something is happening," Carvin whispered. "My father has had soldiers running everywhere all day."

"Something?" Jackie asked in confusion.

"Remember when I told you about the Temple of Adherency and the dwarf that controls it?" Carvin asked. When she nodded he continued. "There's a rebellion stirring around the Lakes. Word has begun to filter back to my father and the leader of the Temple on Manitoulin Island of what has happened. Apparently the rebels are led by a young woman from the other side of the Divide who looks a lot like you."

"Jane!" Jackie gasped. "But how could she have come here?"

"There are people who can pass back and forth," Carvin admitted.

"Why didn't you tell me that before?" Jackie asked in a hurt voice.

"Because it is rare," Carvin said as he defended himself. "Without the aid of a talented map maker and someone who knows how to craft the anchors it is nearly impossible. I didn't want to get your hopes up until I found someone who was willing to help us escape."

"Wait a minute, help us escape?" Jackie said. She arched one eyebrow at him and waited for him to continue.

"Well, I was hoping to escape with you," Carvin admitted. His face turned red as he stammered over the words. "I hate this place and I hate my father. He's horrible, you've seen what he did to me last time he caught me coming to visit you. I would join the rebellion if I thought I had a way to escape the Isle of Lakes."

"So what do we do?" Jackie asked. She huddled on the edge of her bed and whispered the words softly, trying to make sure she would not be heard outside the cell. Suddenly from outside the room there was a chorus of shouts and Carvin's face paled.

122

"I'll be back for you," Carvin hissed. He rose and hurried to the door. "I promise you, we are going to escape this place tonight. I don't know how yet but I'm not letting you stay in this cell any longer."

A look of determination filled his face, and for the first time in almost a year Jackie felt a sense of hope. Maybe, just maybe, she would finally escape this place and return to her own world.

CHAPTER SIXTEEN

Reunion

JANE WALKED UP the wide stone steps to the fortress under the watchful eyes of dozens of Adherents in crisp uniforms, each carrying the newest version of the magic musket. Unlike the Adherents she had seen up until then, these soldiers were professionals and showed no signs of weakness. Stern faces watched her, but their eyes widened slightly at the sight of her escort and no one dared to interrupt them.

"This way, my dear," Averill said. They turned right after entering the imposing fortress. Thick stone walls almost thirty feet tall guarded the outside and three buildings, forming an open sided square, and filled the area to the right of the gate. To the left and before the gates a sprawling series of buildings, all connected to each other, filled the open area where Jane could see dozens of people moving about. Many of those inside the walls wore the black robes of the Adherency but some were dressed in brighter colors.

"Who are they?" Jane asked pointing to the men and women all wearing white robes. Their skin was olive color and their hair almost completely black without exception.

"A group of clerics from the Persian Zoroastrians," Averill said as he motioned for her to continue walking. "They came here from half way around the world to see Overmaster Cain's factories and to bargain for his science."

Averill led Jane to the middle of the three buildings and entered through an open gate. The first room was a massive vaulted affair with many soldiers standing guard over a half dozen tables with stacks of papers and worried men and women studying them. One glance at Averill, and they motioned him through the maze towards a staircase that led down. As far as Jane could see, the stairs continued into the ground, but Averill had her exit on the first floor. The tunnel was well lit, and a barred gate blocked their progress. A stern soldier stood nearby.

"I have a special prisoner," Averill said to the dwarf fingering his pistol-like weapon and watching them.

The soldier looked at Jane with an appraising stare before he keyed open the door and allowed them to enter the passage. Two more dwarf soldiers waited for them beyond the gate, and they guided Jane towards a distant cell protected with an iron door. When they arrived, Averill stepped forward and tapped the iron with his knuckle.

"You know what this is?" Averill asked.

"Iron?" Jane replied.

"Not just iron. But cold iron. It's nearly immune to magic," Averill explained. "Your skill as a Map Maker is useless inside here. Of course you understand the dangers of trying to cross over without an anchor or a map. Death . . . lost forever in the darkness of the Divide."

One of the dwarf escorts opened the door and motioned for her to step inside.

"Besides, when Cain receives the report I'm going to file, he'll bring you both to Lake Huron to see him," Averill said with a shrug.

"I thought you said you wouldn't turn me over," Jane said accusingly.

"Oh, I won't. But I'm sure the master of this island will," Averill said with a smug laugh.

The other dwarf gave her a shove, and she fell into the cell. The door was slammed shut, and the key turned with a loud clunk. Jane glared at the door as she came to her feet, but a sound from the far side of the cell drew her attention, and she turned to face the other person in the cell.

"JANE!"

Jane turned and was nearly bowled over as her sister, Jackie, wrapped her in a great hug. Tears streamed down both of their faces as they clung to each other. After almost a year of not knowing what had happened, Jane was overjoyed to see her sister again, and the joy of the reunion overshadowed their dire circumstances.

"I missed you so much," Jane whispered as she stepped back with her hands on her sister's shoulders. "When you vanished from the university, everyone said you were kidnapped or dead. I never believed it." She examined her sister closely looking for any sign of mistreatment. Despite the long absence from their world, Jackie was still a raven-haired beautiful young woman. Their faces were nearly the same with high cheek bones and a look that many people said reminded them of a young Jackie

Kennedy. Her raven hair was pulled back into a rough pony tail, and her clothing was thread bare and smudged, but she had managed to keep it clean despite all she had been through.

"How did you get here?" Jackie asked. She sat down on the rough bunk nearby and motioned for Jane to sit next to her. "I didn't think anyone would be ever able to find me. Heck, I thought I had gone insane when I came to and saw that black-robed freak looking down at me."

"You must have been terrified," Jane said sympathetically. She looked around but discounted any attempt to escape through the Divide. Even if they had anchors, the cell was lined on all sides with cold iron and would rebuff any attempt at escape.

"For a while I was scared, confused, exhausted." Jackie admitted. "Then I slowly started to understand this place. I began to realize what it was, and that helped me hold on to my sanity. Under better circumstances, it'd really be amazing to visit this place. The other prisoners I talked to describe the natural beauty of this island so vividly, it was hard to see how anyone would want to destroy it."

"The same could be said for our side," Jane muttered with a sad shake of her head. "I mean, don't get me wrong, I enjoy the comforts of life as much as anyone, but those people purposefully destroy things. . ." She shook her head. "It's just wrong."

"So what do we do now?" Jackie asked. "I keep hearing whispered rumors between some of the other prisoners of a rebellion. We have to keep our voices down though because the guards beat anyone who speaks about it." Jackie pulled up the corner of her shirt and showed Jane a nasty black bruise that covered the middle of her back. "One of the short ones hit me with a thick club one day for saying something too loud. It still hurts."

Jane's eyes narrowed as she fumed angrily. "Somehow Tasker will figure out something. I hope anyway."

"Who's Tasker?" Jackie asked curiously. She kept her voice low so that no one outside of the cell stood any chance of hearing them.

"He's the dwarf who came and found me," Jane explained. "He was training me to be a Map Maker and showed me what I can do."

"A dwarf?" Jackie muttered. "Huh, that's weird."

"What?" Jane asked.

"Well," Jackie paused. "One of the other prisoners who's been here for a while said he overheard Blumm Dragrog, the commander of Viscount Lerod's soldiers, laughing about what he called the 'supposed rebellion' and the fact that one of their own short ones was guiding it."

"It can't be Tasker," Jane scoffed. "He was on our side of the Divide for the last fifteen years searching for Jacob and me."

"Yeah. You're right," Jackie admitted. "It doesn't sound like he could be guiding a rebellion from our world." Jackie was silent a few minutes, in awe that after a year of separation they were back together. "I must admit there's only one reason they keep me here. The Viscount's son likes me, he even whispered once that he was working on trying to find a way to help me escape."

"How do you know he isn't trying to set you up?" Jane whispered back. She looked around nervously.

"He isn't," Jackie replied with a nervous smile.

"You like him?" Jane said in surprise. "That's like dating the enemy."

"No one chooses their parents," Jackie said back to her. "And Carvin is nothing like his father. He's kind and sweet and wants nothing to do with the Temple of Adherency. His father's a vicious brute who had his own wife murdered. Carvin wants to leave this place behind and go somewhere far away where the Adherents can't find him."

"And you'd go with him?" Jane asked. Now that the initial shock had passed, she could see Jackie was seriously considering staying.

"Well, I had nothing more to look forward to until now," Jackie replied with a shrug. "I was stuck here with no real prospects of ever going home. Now I'm not sure."

There was a scuffle beyond the door to the cell. Moments later the thick iron portal opened, and a tall young man with wide shoulders slipped inside, followed by four Adherents carrying a second bunk and two trays of food.

"I brought your meal," he said but then his voice trailed off. He stayed silent until the others left and then looked from Jackie to Jane. He began to understand the situation once he saw how much they looked alike. "Jane, I presume?"

"Carvin, this is my sister," Jackie said. Before they could say anything more, a shout of anger outside the door drew their attention, and a mountain of man threw open the iron door.

"Carvin, get out of there!"

Jackie skittered back, pulling Jane with her. She intoned to Jane, "The man's a brute. Several times I believed he was going to force me into his bed, but, thankfully I managed to avoid it each time."

"The little brat has a sister, huh?" the Viscount roared with a vile grin that spoke volumes. He crossed to where Jane sat and grabbed her chin in his hand. An iron grip forced her head up until she was staring at him. "Maybe I'll come for both of you later. You should be thankful Master Cain has ordered that anyone captured from the other side be kept intact until he decides what to do with them." He roared a coarse laugh and stepped back to where Carvin was huddled in a corner, trying to avoid being seen.

"And you," Viscount Lerod snarled. He cuffed his son hard on the back of the head. The blow sent him reeling into the wall. "What a pathetic excuse for an offspring. I'm glad I had the wench that birthed you killed. If I didn't need an heir, I'd have you follow in her footsteps, but I keep hoping you'll wake up to what we have here."

"Yes, father," Carvin muttered as he picked himself off the floor and brushed off the dirt.

"Our spies report there are rebels about," Viscount Lerod said. "I want you to rouse two companies and make sure they're ready to respond to any attack. Four hundred soldiers should be more than sufficient to respond to anything these supposed rebels can muster. Have them board their ships and be ready to set sail when we track down their location."

"Yes, father," Carvin replied. He cast a worried look at Jackie, then rushed from the cell to the barracks buildings on either side, where many of the fortress's three thousand soldiers were housed.

Back inside the prison cell, Jane wiped her face as the Viscount stepped out of the cell and slammed the door behind him. The key turned in the lock again and once more she and her sister were alone.

"All right," Jane muttered, feeling violated just from his stares. "Carvin seems nice, but his father needs to be put down like a rabid dog."

Still her heart leapt at the thought of Tasker and the others coming to her aid. How they would do it was beyond her, but she hoped it was true.

"Do you really think someone's coming for you?" Jackie asked.

"For *us*, Jackie," Jane replied. "Yes. I think they're coming for us. I'll never leave you behind, no matter what happens."

They sat on their crude bunks talking about what happened. Jane told her story in hushed tones that no one could overhear. The meal was plain but filling, and despite the fact it was cold it tasted fine. With no windows, they had no idea what time it was. When the dwarf guard returned for their trays, he refused to tell Jane about the time.

When they grew tired of talking, they pulled their bunks close to each other and lay down to sleep. Jane was still amazed she'd found her sister after a year of believing she was gone forever. Her mind whirled as she tried to sleep in the dark cell, but remained wide awake listening and hoping for help.

* * * * *

TASKER AND ERIUNIA WALKED slowly down the twisted streets of the Isle of Lakes. Much of the southern half of the island was covered with the industrial complex that fed the massive shipyard. They had left the ore ship as it pulled into a small dock south of the main shipyard. A forest of smoke stacks and rough cranes blocked their view of whatever was being built. Despite being curious about what the ore ship captain had hinted, Eriunia knew their main goal was the freeing of Jane and Jackie, and they needed to stay focused on that. Braun and three others trailed them at a discreet distance, not wanting to draw attention to a large group. They all wore Adherent robes, but Eriunia was beginning to notice subtle differences between the robes they wore and those worn by those few Adherents around them.

"It's going to give us away," she said to Tasker when she pointed out that their robes were older and lacked the symbols of the others. "I think some of us would blend in better without the robes." She motioned back out to the street. They stood in a dark alley, while Braun kept watch at the entrance.

Tasker agreed. "Have those following us remove their robes."

The nearby fortress wall had a thirty-foot empty space between it and the surrounding city. Far to the west, the sun was disappearing beyond wooded hills as they made their way quickly to the last house separating them from the fortress.

"Up you go," Braun hoisted the first man up the side of the stone building and then boosted the second one up. When they were all standing on the wood and tar roof, they walked quickly to the side facing the fortress. "Now we wait."

"How long will it take?" Eriunia asked. Suddenly, from the western half of the city a loud flapping of wings and the flash of a dark form knifed through the air. Then a line of liquid fire rained down on the city, setting fire to the wooden roofs and drawing screams from the horrified people. "What was that?"

"I don't know, but it's working in our favor," Tasker said, pointing to where the watchful soldiers were racing to the far walls to see the fires. Five minutes later the southern wall was empty, and Braun stood openly on the rooftop as he launched a thin but strong rope across the space. It fell perfectly across a section of the wall that stuck up above the others and held tightly when he pulled against it.

"Here we go," Braun said as he checked his weapons and tied off the near end of the rope. "Remember to untie the rope when we are inside." The rebel soldiers nodded and crouched down next to the rope. "Tasker, good luck with your part." He waved to them then went hand over hand across the space and slipped over the wall.

"Be safe," Tasker said to Eriunia as she started across the rope.

She looked back at him and nodded, "You also." He had been tight lipped about his part of the plan, but Eriunia thought it included finding out what was being built inside the shipyard and trying to cause some havoc on the docks before their planned retreat. Moments later, she slipped off the edge of the wall to crouch next to Braun. The third and fourth members of their rescue party followed, and they pulled the rope across. Tasker and the last rebel then headed west—the escape now in their hands.

"The ship captain said he'd been inside the fortress once to pick up a crew member who had been taken into custody," Braun explained as they overlooked the brooding fortress. In a flurry of activity soldiers opened the main gate further west and a broad column of soldiers marched out. Below them they saw the three buildings that marked the dungeon's entrance and watched for signs of movement. Suddenly their eyes were drawn to furtive shadows next to the wall below them.

"Is that who I think it is?" Eriunia hissed suddenly. She pointed to the figures crouched below them against the barracks' wall. Along the back of the structure, out of sight from the last of the soldiers, Jacob and Flying Cloud, with Bella perched atop Jacob's shoulder, dashed across the open space and disappeared into the dungeon entrance.

"What do we do?" Braun asked, looking to Eriunia. All of them carried bows instead of magic muskets because it was hard to be stealthy when a glowing trail of energy followed every shot you fired.

"We wait and help them escape," Eriunia said without hesitation. "We can cover them from here well enough and have our ropes ready to climb down the moment they emerge. Braun, go guide them to us."

The elf soldier nodded and shimmied down a rope held by the other two soldiers. Eriunia watched until he disappeared into the dungeon, then motioned for the other two soldiers to ready themselves. "Make sure the ropes are tied off. Then spread out and be ready."

They nodded and turned to fix three lengths of rope to the wall, letting them dangle down the far side. All three crouched in the shadow cast by the wall, bows ready and arrows clenched in their fists.

"Uh oh," Eriunia muttered. "Trouble."

Three men crossed the courtyard coming from the fortress. One was young, maybe eighteen or twenty years at most and dressed unlike any other Adherent she had seen. He carried a leather pack and was armed with a pistol, a rifle and a sword. He seemed nervous as he walked slightly behind the other two Adherents.

"Stay here and cover us," Eriunia whispered to the other two rebels. She flipped her bow over her shoulder and shimmied down the rope into the courtyard.

CHAPTER SEVENTEEN

Passing of a Friend

A SCUFFLE OF BOOTS and a stifled shout outside the door brought Jane and Jackie to their feet. They clung to each other in the darkness as they waited. A rattle of keys continued for some time as the person outside the door searched for the right one. When the portal finally swung open, Jane squealed in delight as Flying Cloud and Bella stepped into the cell and looked around. Despite her earlier feelings about the other girl, she had never been happier to see someone in her life.

"Flying Cloud! Bella!" Jane quietly exclaimed, but she caught herself, not wanting to alert anyone . "What are you doing here?"

"Jane, what are you doing here?" Flying Cloud asked, almost as surprised.

"Jane?" Jacob asked from the door. He looked nervously up and down the passage outside the cells and then back in at her in surprise. "What are you doing here?"

"Is there an echo in here?" Bella asked suddenly as she flapped her one good wing.

"But . . ." Jacob started.

"I think we should save the explanations for later," Flying Cloud piped as she motioned towards the door. "We don't know how long we have before someone comes to check on the dungeons."

"You're right," Jane said grudgingly. She grabbed Jackie's hand and pulled her towards the open door. "Come on. We're getting out of here."

"I wish I could say goodbye to Carvin," Jackie said. She followed Jane into the hallway and crouched next to her as Jacob hurriedly explained.

"Yerdarva is creating a disturbance for us," Jacob explained. "We need to get back out the gate before anything happens to her." He turned and led them back to the dungeon entrance. They all hurried through the door but skidded to a halt. Spread out in the big room were ten black-robed Adherents. Averill stood in the center of the group with his pistol drawn, a grin on his face.

"So, the traitor was right," Averill said with a laugh. "And you walked right into our hands with your eyes wide open." He looked around suddenly as he counted those crouched next to Jacob. "Where's the other one? Our sources told us four were coming into the dungeon, which should have totaled six not five."

"Who betrayed us?" Jacob muttered angrily.

"Oh, wouldn't you like to know, boy," Averill laughed. "I think I'll keep that bit of information for Cain to explain to you when you stand before him."

Jacob raised his shield and readied himself for what he knew was coming. It was impossible for him to stop all the magic muskets shots, but he might be able to buy the others time to escape into the passage behind him and bar the door.

"Don't even try, boy," Averill said in a low voice. "Your shield may stop some of our shots, but it can't stop all of them. There's no other escape from the dungeons. One way out and one way in."

A whisper of sound came from the shadows, and one of the Adherents cried out and fell to the floor, an arrow sticking from his neck.

"What in the seven hells," Averill started as his men looked about. Five of the Adherents clustered together with their backs to each other searching the shadows for the invisible attacker.

Another flash of movement, and then Jacob saw the familiar form of Braun erupt from the shadows with a stolen musket held low and trained on the five. He triggered the weapon, and the ball of energy crackled wildly as it flashed across the room and sent all five tumbling to the floor with their muscles twitching and surprised looks painted across their faces.

"Elf!" Averill cried out. Rage filled his face. "Don't shoot him. This one is mine!" He leapt forward and knocked the musket from one of the Adherent's hands.

"Assassin," Braun said with a grim smile. He spat on the floor and pulled a sword from his belt, its blade etched with black lines and flared with barely contained power. Averill's own blade was steel, but the edge appeared black as if it might be partially obsidian.

"Are you ready to die?" Averill asked.

"I should ask the same of you, assassin," Braun said with an easy smile. Their blades flashed with impossible speed as they lashed out at each other. Sparks of power erupted at each meeting of the weapons, and they weaved a battle of such power everyone gazed on in awe. Averill was the picture of power and savage fury as he struck with all his might time after time, forcing Braun to give ground.

Braun smiled thinly as he turned aside blow after blow and slipped away each time the assassin thought he was trapped. The other blade destroyed tables with a single blow and harsh kicks sent the section of furniture into his path to try and trip him, but Braun easily avoided the obstacles. He had lived this type of battle a thousand times, honing his muscles and reactions until they came as naturally as breathing. He was outmatched in strength, and he knew it, so he relied on his reflexes and the natural grace of his body as he met the fury of the beast and turned it away.

"What's going on here?"

The surprised shout stopped all movement for a heartbeat and Braun used the distraction to slip his sword under Averill's guard and land a slashing blow against the other's side. He knew he was going to pay for the strike as he accepted the smashing blow from the other's free hand. Rolling with the force of the strike, he managed to lessen the ringing in his head and return to his feet with a small trickle of blood running from his nose.

"Carvin," Averill shouted as he clutched the wound on his side. It hurt worse than he would let the elf know, while his own blow seemed to have barely rattled his opponent. "Sound the alarm. They're trying to free the prisoners."

"Carvin!" Jackie cried aloud. "Please help us."

The son of the viscount stood frozen as the two men with him pulled their muskets and joined the remaining Adherents trying to cover everyone with their weapons. He looked over to the pile of Adherents collapsed to the floor still unconscious from the blast of energy. The viscount was out leading the defense against the fires now threatening to destroy a large section of the city. Fires, Carvin knew, were aided by men loyal to him alone. He looked up at Jackie and could not fight the fact that he was in love with her. He didn't know if she felt the same, but he knew there was nothing for him here, nothing but the abusive rants of a father who hated him.

"I'm sorry," Carvin muttered as he stared at Jackie. He noticed Averill's face lit up, thinking he was apologizing to her for betraying her. Slowly he pulled both his pistol and his musket and leveled them across the room with steady hands at the man about his own age holding the red shield. Carvin saw him grimace and crouch behind the shield, trusting in it to protect him from what he knew was coming. "I'm truly sorry," Carvin said again, but this time his eyes flickered once to Averill. He saw the assassin's eyes widen as he shifted his musket ever so slightly and pulled the trigger. The ball of energy caught Averill square in the chest and sent him flying backwards into the wall. Carvin swung his pistol across and blasted the man standing beside him at such close range that he felt the numbing effect of the energy tingle across his hands and nearly dropped his pistol. The weapon contained four more charges, and he quickly rotated the cylinder and fired a shot that made one more Adherent crumple to the ground.

Shouts of alarm erupted from those still standing, and Carvin ducked behind the remains of a table as the Adherents cried traitor.

Braun nearly laughed as Averill went flying. He charged the cluster of Adherents still standing and went through them with his sword flashing. Suddenly the room went silent, and Braun looked over to Jacob. "Are you all right?"

"I think we all are," Jacob said as he reached back and helped Jane to her feet. He thought he saw a flash of something in Flying Cloud's eyes, but his attention was drawn away.

"Get some of the muskets. We should move," Braun said. "We made enough noise to wake the dead."

Jacob retrieved several of the muskets and handed them to each of the women. Jane already knew how to use the weapon, and she took over showing Jackie and Flying Cloud how to arm the weapon and fire it.

"How did you know we were going to be here?" Jacob asked Braun.

"We didn't," Braun muttered. "Jane was taken by the assassin, and we were trying to rescue her. What worries me more is that, if the turncoat Adherent hadn't helped us out, we would probably all be locked in a cell. The Brotherhood assassin was one of their best. I am not sure how much longer I would have been able to stay ahead of him."

"I'm not a turncoat!" Carvin blustered as he emerged from behind the destroyed table and then stopped. "Well, maybe I am but . . ."

"I'm not complaining," Braun replied. "All right, let's move."

They all walked to the main door leading out into the fortress. Jane nervously gripped the musket. The weapon felt heavy in her hands, but she ran through the way she had been trained to arm it and knew it was ready. The courtyard between the three buildings was quiet, and they emerged and hurried towards the waiting ropes. Carvin was jogging next to Jackie, talking to her in hushed tones, and she smiled up at him several times.

"Something's wrong," Braun said as they neared the barracks building that blocked them from the wall.

Jane was about to answer when a shrill scream broke the silence of the night, and they all skidded to a halt. Around them in a rush of movement, scores of Adherents in black robes erupted from their hiding places and rushed to surrounded them. Viscount Lerod stepped outwards them, dragging the struggling form of Eriunia with him, his iron grip around her arm.

"So, my own offspring betrays me and sides with the filth of the rebel trash," Viscount Lerod growled. He threw Eriunia down to the ground before him and glared down at her. "What about it, elf. I don't think we even need a trial. I sentence you to death for crimes against the temple." He picked up one of the new style weapons and armed it. "You know what's the best thing about these new muskets?" He worked some of the setting on the side of the weapon and then pointed it at Eriunia, who had rolled back until she was about ten feet from where Braun stood. "Instead of only stunning, we can set them to completely overload the target's nervous system. I shoot you with it set on the highest setting, and your body will shut down. I saw one live target suffocate to death after being shot in the chest." He aimed the weapon at Eriunia and laughed. "Goodbye, elf."

Braun lunged forward in a flash and rolled his body in front of Eriunia. The jolt of energy that struck him was twice the size of anything Jane had seen before, and she saw the look of shock that filled Braun's face. The blast rolled out around him, but Eriunia was shielded from the worst of it and managed to crawl to his body when it landed.

"You monster," Eriunia cried. She cradled Braun's head in her arms and shook his shoulders. "Please, Braun, don't die. I can't do this alone."

"I'm sorry my princess," Braun managed to gasp as his body shook uncontrollably. "I tried." With those words his eyes glazed over and lost focus. A moment later his lungs rattled violently and his breathing stopped.

Jane stared in shock down at the body of the elf warrior who had so skillfully led the rebels across the decks of the Ironships and had been such a help in such a short time. In a jostling of movement the Adherents pushed forward. Jackie, Jacob, and Carvin were all clustered nearby with their muskets still pointed outwards. Jane grabbed Eriunia by the shoulders and pulled her back from Braun's body. Flying Cloud was crouched near Jacob's feet, and Jane could see her fingers moving. She shoved both hands inside her bandolier bag and seemed to be ready to carry on the fight.

"Make her stop, or I'll shoot her too," Viscount Lerod growled as he leveled his rifle on Flying Cloud.

Jacob stepped in front of her with his shield held before him, "I will kill you if it's the last thing I ever do."

"Good luck, boy," Viscount Lerod laughed as he pulled the trigger. A great ball of energy flashed across the space between them and struck the shield. Instead of knocking Jacob to the ground, the flash of energy pulsed out around the small group and washed over the Adherents behind them. The viscount's eyes widened as eight of his men crumbled to the ground and lay trembling uncontrollably.

Jacob angled his shield as he saw the rage forming in the viscount's face, and he managed to direct the blasts of energy away from them and across the Adherents. The effects were almost instantaneous—many of them fell to the ground, knocked senseless by the energy while others turned and fled.

"Bah, worthless weapon," Viscount Lerod roared. He threw the rifle to the ground and pulled a massive broadsword from the sheath at his side.

Jane saw him rush Jacob, and she saw Jacob raise his shield against a tremendous overhand blow. Sparks erupted from the shield, and Jacob cried out in pain as he was driven back and thrown to the ground. Chaos erupted around her, and Carvin began to methodically pick off the Adherents still on their feet. Wild shots from Jackie's musket careened off the buildings and added to the confusion. Here and there Adherents threw up their hands and slumped to the ground as feathered shafts flashed out of the night and struck them with perfect precision. Jane turned to see the viscount raising his massive sword once again, and Jacob struggled to raise his shield. Jacob's sword lay on the ground at her feet. Jane leaned over to pick it up.

"Time to die, boy," Viscount Lerod said with a deep, booming laugh. Suddenly his eyes went wide and he gasped in pain.

Jane pushed the blade into the viscount's back as hard as she could. She heard him start to laugh at Jacob and then stop. The sword went in slowly, and she shoved with all her might, sending it completely through him. To her surprise he did not fall to the ground but instead turned slowly to face her.

"You little brat," Viscount Lerod muttered. His sword slumped to the ground on arms that no longer had the strength to hold it. He clutched around his back trying to grab the weapon and remove it but finally gave up and grabbed Jane's shoulders. "I can still kill you."

Jane pushed as hard as she could against the iron grip but found she was trapped against it. Ever so slowly Viscount Lerod pulled her towards the tip of the sword sticking through the front of his chest. Suddenly he stiffened once again, and the strength completely left his arms. Jane managed to pull away. The bloody blade had been an inch from her chest.

"This is for my mother," Carvin whispered in his estranged father's ear. "I hope you burn forever for what you did to her." He pushed his belt knife in until it finally found the still beating heart of the man who claimed to be his father. The claim may have been true but in Carvin's mind he had no father, only a mother who had loved him unconditionally.

Slowly the viscount tumbled to the ground face first and lay there without moving. The courtyard was quiet for the first time, and Jane looked around her at the general destruction.

"We should go," Carvin muttered finally. He picked up the rifle his father had thrown aside and turned the setting back to stun.

"I agree," Jacob said as he stood up and tried to move his shoulder. He winced as the partially dislocated joint popped back into place.

The five of them hurried to the wall where the two rebels waited, guarding the ropes that were their only escape. There was a rustle of wind and a rush of movement, and Yerdarva landed on the wall nearby and looked at them. Jane saw blood and streaks of black on her hide but the dragon seemed still spoiling for the fight.

"You need to go quickly," Yerdarva cried. She paused to send a line of liquid flame into the gate house and block the rush of Adherents who were trying to level their weapons at her. "The fire from the ships I cannot withstand, and they're starting to find their ranges." To punctuate her words, a roar of energy and a massive ball of magical power struck a nearby building. Moments later two more conventional iron cannon balls smashed into the walls near the gate house and sent bits of rock flying high into the air.

"I'll clear you a path to the west," Yerdarva said as she jumped down into the courtyard and engulfed one of the barracks buildings completely in fire. "Take one of the smaller ships and flee. We have struck a hard blow today, and it won't go unnoticed."

"Thank you," Jacob said to her as he helped the others climb down the ropes to the streets below.

"Do not waste this chance," Yerdarva said. "It'll take me many days to replenish my energy, so you won't see me again for some time." With those words she leapt up and took to the air as flames roared out of control throughout the barracks and the fortress.

CHAPTER EIGHTEEN

Running the Divide

FOLLOW ME," Carvin said. "I can lead you through the backstreets to a boat big enough for all of us."

"He's still an Adherent," Jacob muttered as he let go of the rope and glared at Carvin. "Why should we trust him?"

"He just helped stop his own father, Jacob," Jane replied with a shake of her head. "He just saved my life."

"You heard the assassin," Jacob shot back. "Someone betrayed the rebellion and told them that Eriunia and others were coming today. Who else knew?"

"This is hardly the time for long-winded explanations," Carvin said calmly. He pointed to the castle wall and continued. "They're not going to wait long to begin searching for us." Another round of cannon fire roared overhead, chasing after the swooping form of Yerdarva as she turned entire streets into masses of liquid fire.

"Come on. Tasker can find us on his own," Jane said as she motioned for Carvin to take the lead. She took Jacob's hand and pulled him along. "Come on. We don't have time to discuss this right now." Behind them Flying Cloud and Eriunia were standing close to each other, and Jane thought she saw a twinge of jealousy in the other girl's eyes. The last two rebels were coming down the ropes now and a scattering of shouts came from inside the fortress.

Jane followed Carvin as he hurried from street to alley, taking a moment to look around each corner before rushing headlong out into the open. They passed through areas where the fires still raged wildly out of control and brigades of people pumped water from wells, trying to contain the flames. Hurried looks and calls for help followed them, but they steadfastly held to their course and were soon overlooking a short dock sticking out in the water. The lake was calm despite the chaos around them. Tied to the dock was a large fishing vessel with a small mast and enough room for all of them to stand on the deck.

"Hurry," Carvin said. He motioned for all them to them jump across the space while he cut the rope holding the vessel against the pier. He gave a hard shove as he launched his own body across the growing gap and then reached up and untied the leather straps holding the sail in place. Immediately the breeze moving across the water caught the thick canvas cloth and pulled them away from the shore.

"What about Tasker," Jane asked. She didn't want the short leader of the rebellion to be trapped on shore.

"I think he has a different plan to escape," Eriunia replied. The wind pushed them west, and they stayed with the breeze, trying to make the run to shore as quickly as they could. They were over half way to the lake shore when the first signs of trouble appeared behind them on the water.

"Ironship coming into view," Eriunia shouted suddenly. She pointed back to where the massive iron vessel was powering through the water towards them. "They're closing on us way too fast."

"I agree. I don't think we can outrun them," Carvin muttered. "We might end up swimming the last hundred yards."

"The water is a little cold for that," Jacob replied with a shake of his head. "Without something to keep us warm, we'd never make it."

"We may not have a choice," Carvin said. Suddenly there was a massive roar from the distant ship, and a great plume of water erupted next to them as the cannon ball struck the lake and bounded across the water.

"Jane, here," Eriunia pulled the map and pen from her pocket and handed them to Jane. "Go. Save your sister. Tasker said the anchors are attached to the map. Jacob still has his ring. All of you can be safe."

"No. We're not leaving you until we know everyone's safe," Jane retorted. She took her map fondly and tucked it half way into her pocket.

"I wonder if I can take someone with me through the Divide?" Jacob said suddenly. There was another loud crack, and Carvin yanked the wheel to the right, trying to throw off the aim of the gunners behind them. This time the cannon ball cut through the air overhead and skipped along the shore until it impacted a granite ledge and exploded with a massive ball of fire.

"Try it with me first," Bella piped up as she hurried to where Jacob was standing. She held out her arms to him and waited to be picked up.

"Are you sure about this?" Jane said as she watched Jacob pick up the fairy. His face was set and his eyes hard with determination.

"If we stay here much longer they'll have our range, and it won't make a difference," Jacob replied. "We die here or we die in the water. Your map doesn't reach to this area, but my anchor is still on Tasker's map."

Jane wrapped her arms around him once and gave him a long hug. When she broke away, she nodded and said, "Good luck."

"Hold on tight," Jacob said to Bella. As he vanished into the Divide, he heard the cannon bark again. This time a great spray of water erupted, and shouts of alarm came from those still on board the fishing vessel.

"Uph," Jacob grunted as the darkness of the Divide closed in around them and seemed to be physically battling them both. He could feel his strength sapping as he dove headlong through the grand map before him and fell with a thud to the rocky ground. They had jumped less than five hundred yards and still he felt winded.

"Get under cover," he told Bella. "I will be right back."

"Good luck," Bella shouted as she ran to the shelter of the strong cliffs beyond the shore.

The return through the Divide was a test of skill and aim as the small craft bobbed and jumped about the surface of Lake Superior. As it was, he ended up emerging from the blackness about a foot above the deck of the boat and falling to the hard deck planks.

"Who's next," Jacob said as he stood and looked around.

"Take Jackie," Jane insisted as she pulled her sister over to Jacob.

"No someone else," Jackie tried to protest, but Jane silenced her.

"I lost you once," Jane said fiercely. "I'm not losing you again."

"Take her," Carvin shouted. "I can make the swim if need be."

Jacob nodded and wrapped his arms around Jackie as tightly as he could, "Hold on to me. This may get rough." He was acutely aware of her beauty and how warm her skin was as he willed them both into the Divide, but he pushed the feeling aside. He was confused enough with Jane and Flying Cloud. He hardly needed to develop feelings for anyone else. This time the Divide howled in protest as he forced his way through the map and fell to the ground near where he had dropped Bella. This time he felt like he just finished sprinting a mile.

"Go up the hill," Jacob said to Jackie as he released his grip on her. "Bella's there. She'll help you." He pointed up the hill and his hand shook slightly. Moments later he was falling to the deck of the fishing vessel once again. This time the booming report of a cannon from the closing Ironship sent the cannon ball smashing through the mast and sent it flying into the lake. Flying Cloud was crouched on the deck close by, and Jacob grabbed her and pulled her close. As he entered the Divide again he saw the pained look on Jane's face, but then they were gone, and all he could feel was Flying Cloud pressed against him. This time it was all he could do to force his way out of the darkness. They both fell to the ground with a shout of surprise.

"There," Jacob gasped as he pointed up the hill to where Jackie and Bella were crouched behind a thick outcropping of granite. She leaned over and kissed him once before letting go and scrambed up the hill and out of sight. And again Jacob went into the blackness. Traveling through the Divide was nearly impossible this time, and when he finally managed to find the fishing vessel, he fell to the deck of this ship and lay panting.

BOOM!

The Ironship guns spoke, and this time Jacob heard the whistling of the cannon ball just before it struck the bow of the ship and sent the vessel lurching drunkenly to the side. Carvin vanished with a surprised look as the vessel began to come apart, and Jacob saw Eriunia leap into the water as a second shot slammed into the rear of the ship. The two rebels who had survived the raid disappeared with only enough time to shout in surprise.

Jane was crouched on the deck near him, her eyes wide with fear.

"Come on, Jane," Jacob shouted. "We can make it through one more time."

"Do you like her?" Jane asked as she stumbled to where he lay on the deck. She threw herself down next to him as a third cannon ball roared overhead and narrowly missed the remaining section of the vessel that was somehow still floating. They were sinking slowly, and Jane felt the cold water slip around her feet.

"What?" Jacob said as he looked at her.

"Do you like her?" Jane repeated. She rolled over and stared into his eyes, thinking about how much she had liked them the first time they met.

"Who?" Jacob asked in bewilderment.

"Flying Cloud," Jane replied. It was as though the lake around them had gone silent and all that remained was the two of them sitting on the raft and drifting through the water.

"Well, yes . . . well, I don't know . . ." Jacob stammered. He cared for both of them and couldn't make up his mind which he liked better. "I like you a lot, Jane . . . but I like her a lot too." He shook his head. "I wish I had never come here."

Jane started to pull back. The words hurt her more then she could say. He must have seen the betrayal in her eyes because he reached out to her and stopped her from pulling away.

"Not when I came back for you," Jacob explained. "I wish we had just stayed in Duluth and gone to get our ice cream. Just the two of us. No Adherents, no maps, nothing else, just us together. I mean I'm happy we found your sister. I just wish things were simple again."

Jane smiled at him. "I guess maybe I just need to prove to you that I'm the better woman." She looked up and saw the bow of the Ironship closing in quickly, its cannons pointed directly at them. Great search lights lit the water, and for a moment she thought she saw a flash of metal underneath the waves. She wrapped herself into Jacob's grip as tightly as she could and nodded to him.

"Ready?" Jacob asked.

"I'm ready," Jane replied. She reached her lips up and kissed him as they entered the Divide.

Jacob felt the darkness slam into them like a massive wave seeking to drown them in its depths. He fought and struggled against it, but he could feel his grip on the real world slipping away. He and Jane were a step from being swept away forever into the grasp of the great Divide. Then he felt Jane's warm lips touch his again.

"If I'm going to be lost forever in darkness," Jane whispered in his ear, "then I'm going to be lost forever with you."

Moments later they emerged from the Divide and fell to the ground with a thud that broke their embrace and sent them rolling away from each other. They were helped to their feet and guided up the hill and out of sight as the Ironship unleashed its guns one last time on the small fishing boat.

"Wait," Jacob burst out as Flying Cloud tried to pull him away from the lake. "Eriunia and Carvin are in the water." He stumbled almost drunkenly down the rocks to the shore and peered out over the water. He heard the clanging of a warning bell out across the lake, and he looked up to where the Ironship was slowly coming to a halt. Its guns were trying to track out across the water, and Jacob wondered what was happening. Then a dark shadow whipped across the lake, and a line of fire struck the ship, nearly rolling it over.

"Yerdarva!" Jacob shouted. He saw the dragon swoop low to the water and snatch two people from the cold depths. Moments later she dropped them on the shore nearby and turned her head wearily towards them.

"I go to my rest," Yerdarva said. "Use well what you have gained this night. It'll be some time before my strength has returned." Yerderva lifted into the air and pushed west away from the battles and back to her waiting son.

The Ironship was close enough that Jane saw the figures scrambling around the deck, fighting the fires and still trying to bring the cannons in line across the water. She tried to see what they were pointing at. Suddenly the prow of the small submarine broke the surface of the water, and she heard the high pitch whine of a torpedo entering the water. The ship's cannons barked once, but both shots missed horribly. Then the torpedo struck the ship and a great explosion lit the night.

"Kind of a nice light show tonight, isn't it," Jacob said with a chuckle.

"That it is," Eriunia replied with a dry laugh. Her face, though, was pained as she thought about the loss of Braun.

"I assume that's what Tasker was after," Eriunia said as she watched the little underwater vessel turn away from the sinking ruins of the Ironship and make its way towards them.

Their meeting on the shore was mostly happy as they remembered the deeds Braun had done to help them. Even though his body was not present, they commended his spirit to the afterlife. The submarine was cramped, but they all fit into it and slowly made their way across the lake to the south until they arrived back at Madeline Island.

"Almost feels like coming home," Jacob muttered. "How weird."

Jane laughed at him and slipped her arm around his waist before Flying Cloud could even leave the dock. They laughed and sang long into the morning after their return, and then slept the rest of the day and some of the next night. Near midnight Tasker came to where Jacob, Jane, and Jackie were sitting on a hill outside the fortress watching the stars as the night slowly slipped by. Flying Cloud and Bella had gone off into the forest to explore, and Eriunia was inside the fortress.

"She's probably looking over lists of supplies or weapons," Jane said when Jacob pointed out the elf was no longer present.

"Braun's death was hard on her," Tasker said as he walked into view. "Have any of you seen Puck lately?"

"No," Jane replied.

"Who's Puck," Jackie asked, curious.

"Leader of the goblins," Jacob piped in from where he lay on the ground between them.

There was silence for a couple of minutes as Tasker wondered where the short goblin could be. This was a great victory and one that would surely gain Cain's attention. The sacking of the Isle of Lakes would take many months to rebuild. Still, he had seen the massive Iron Goliath sitting in its dry dock. The ship was an abomination, a monster, and he figured it could carry at least a thousand troops. The devastation that would come from its guns would be something no force near it could withstand.

"I made this for you," Tasker said finally to Jackie. He handed her a small anchor that matched the one on Jane's shirt. "It is linked to Jane's map and will allow you to return home safely."

Jackie wrapped the dwarf in a great hug as tears welled in her eyes, "I can't wait to see Mom." Jane had told her how her father had fled back home, and it angered her so much she wished she could tell him what she thought of his leaving.

"We should get back to Grandpa's and call Mom," Jane said. "I think it's better if we get her to drive to Duluth. I don't think this is something we can explain over the phone."

"You're probably right," Jane agreed.

"Let's at least say goodbye to everyone first," Jackie said as she stood and helped Jane up. "I want them to know I'll be coming back to help."

"What!" Jane exclaimed. "I didn't think you would ever want to come here ever again."

"Oh, I owe this Cain character," Jackie growled angrily. "He stole a year of my life and nearly took my hope from me. And I mean to pay him back somehow."

EPILOGUE

"THE ATTACK at the Isle of Lakes has severely damaged our ability to ship iron."

Cain's eyes narrowed in rage, his hands trembling, and his face turning red. He reached up and ripped the anchor from the Adherent's robe and smiled grimly as the man wailed helplessly as he faded into the Divide.

"How badly was the city damaged?" Cain asked the second Adherent who had returned from the Isle of Lakes. The man looked nervously between where his friend had just disappeared and the short leader of the Temple and licked his lips.

"Much of the industrial quarter will have to be rebuilt, sire," he reported. "At least a year before we can return to full production. There was a dragon and land forces. Viscount Lerod was killed and his son is missing. We're not sure if he died in the dragon's fire or was kidnapped by the rebels."

"What of the Iron Goliath?" Cain asked.

"Undamaged. It will be fully operational in a few days," he replied, happy to give his volatile leader some good news.

"And what of the underwater vessel being tested?" Cain asked. He did not address the Adherent this time but the shadows behind him.

"Gone. I was struck by a blast from one of those muskets that your men used and rendered unconscious," Averill muttered. He stepped out of the shadows and ran his dagger into the Adherent killing the man quickly. "And I will finish this job without asking for my usual fee."

"Good," Cain replied as he watched his Adherent drop to the floor. He was done with the man anyway. "Is the damage as bad as he claimed?"

"Yes, unfortunately," Averill nodded as they turned and walked from the room. Outside the building they could see across the grand city Cain had built on Manitoulin Island. Built in the image of what he considered the greatest of cities—the grand Rome. Polished marble columns adorned the buildings, and streets paved with gray marble ran between them. A grand aqueduct brought water from two different rivers on the mainland to fill numerous baths and pools scattered throughout the city. Clay tiled roofs stretched across the city to surround the grand coliseum and over a dozen theaters were scattered around the island. There was no industry here, just the amenities to keep his chosen Adherents happy and content.

"Then it's time to take things into hand personally," Cain muttered. He glanced down distastefully at his hands. "I do so hate interruptions, but I'm beginning to think the Golden Book of Knowledge is not in the new world."

"Where else could they have hidden it?" Averill asked. He was privy to information a select few knew, and Cain's ultimate goal he knew well.

"There are still places where the Temple's grip is very weak," Cain admitted. "We haven't many inroads to the dragon worshippers of the far east. It's hard to penetrate their jungles, and I know my equals have reported the loss of many disciples to the Grand Hierarchy."

"Have you heard anything from the Master of the Temple?" Averill asked. Even though he was not an Adherent, it paid to be well-informed when dealing with an organization of this size and power. There were few places in the world where Temple's tentacles did not reach. He knew that the Temple had started when the first of the dwarves broke through the catacombs under Rome. After such a long isolation under the surface of the world, the dwarves had come bearing amazing things, and their leaders quickly gained great power. Still, it was not a dwarf who guided the Temple to its current position and power. In fact, Averill thought, despite all their sources of information, even the Brotherhood did not know the full makeup of the Grand Hierarchy of the Temple, nor who the Master of the Temple was. Oh, there were rumors and legends but nothing concrete. Suddenly he realized Cain was talking to him, and he pulled his mind back to the present.

"So you and I will go deal with this minor rebellion," Cain said. "First, though, I must send word that our developments on the Goliath are working perfectly. The other members of the Grand Hierarchy will want to copy the designs for their own flagships."

The End
of
The Map Maker's Sister

Coming soon:

The Map Maker's Quest